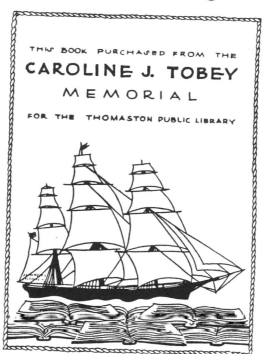

SHORTY

**Center Point
Large Print**

SHORTY

CLIFTON ADAMS

CENTER POINT PUBLISHING

THORNDIKE, MAINE

This Center Point Large Print edition
is published in the year 2005 by arrangement with
Golden West Literary Agency.

The text of this Large Print edition is unabridged. In other
aspects, this book may vary from the original edition. Printed in
Thailand. Set in 16-point Times New Roman type.

ISBN 1-58547-672-2

Library of Congress Cataloging-in-Publication Data

Adams, Clifton.
   Shorty / Clifton Adams.--Center Point large print ed.
      p. cm.
   ISBN 1-58547-672-2 (lib. bdg. : alk. paper)
      1. Large type books. I. Title.

PS3551.D34S56 2005
813'.54--dc22

                                                        2005014331

SHORTY

SHORTY

CHAPTER ONE

1

Shorty Gibbs lay on the gray edge of consciousness, his eyes tightly closed, trying to guess where he was.

A jail cell? Some six-by-six rock calaboose in some nameless trail town? It wouldn't be the *strangest* place he'd ever come alive in.

But wait a minute; he'd stopped trailing back in '85. Or was it '84?

His memory wasn't working so good. His head ached. There was a woolly taste in his mouth and a yawning in his guts. His mind wandered. He got to thinking vaguely about a time in Caldwell when a red-headed saloon girl by the name of Brickyard Floyd . . .

But, hell, he thought disgustedly, that was five, six years ago!

The truth was Shorty Gibbs was just a mite leery of opening his eyes, for fear of what he might see. A big brick furnace, maybe, and a cat-eyed gent with nubbin' horns and red union suit, pitching stiff, cold bodies into the fire with a three-pronged fork. Because, at that moment, Shorty wasn't any too sure that he wasn't dead.

Now, it was beginning to come to him slowly. He had left the old Mobeetee Road, quartering northeast, hoping to finish his mail run at Hardrow before sundown. His pinto must have stepped in a dog hole. The last thing he remembered was flying through the air like a cannonball. The thought of it made him wince. Dog holes and cut banks—the horsebacker's insurance against old age.

A scratchy voice was saying irritably, as if it had already said it several times, "You alive there, mister?"

Cautiously, Shorty Gibbs opened one bloodshot eye. "I ain't right sure," he croaked. He gazed one-eyed at the leathery, bewhiskered face of his host. "Old man," he said finally, "would you mind tellin' me just where I'm at?"

The old-timer shrugged indifferently. "In my wagon—right where you been ever since I hauled you in."

"Hauled me in from where?"

The old man studied his guest thoughtfully. "Well, you was down south a piece when I found you. Not too far from Gyp Creek."

"You see my horse anywheres, a pinto geldin'?"

"Nope." The old-timer turned his head and spat through the puckered opening of the covered wagon.

What could have happened to the pinto? It couldn't have gone far on three legs. "Exactly," Shorty asked with some concern, "how long ago was it that you found me?"

The old man scratched his bristling jaw. "Round three days. If I ain't slipped up somewheres in my figurin'."

Three days! Both eyes were open now, wide. "You sure?"

"Give or take a few hours." Shorty's alarm never scratched the surface of the old man's indifference.

Shorty got his hands under him and shoved with determination. He lurched recklessly to his left and fell against the side boards. "You see anything of my gear?" he panted. "Mail pouch, saddle rifle, war bag?"

"Nope." Hunkered in the rear of the wagon, the old man looked as though he would like to get on with his business, which, from the heady aroma of the wagon, Shorty judged to be sheep. "There was just you," he added grudgingly, "when I seen you. Staggerin' along the creekbank like a Comanche with a bait of 'lectric bitters under his belt."

Shorty blinked and eased himself up on his elbows. "I was on my feet?" It was hard to believe.

"Like I just said. Course, the bullet has laid your scalp open and you was doin' considerable bleedin' . . ."

"Bullet?"

"Boy," the old-timer said impatiently, "you was shot when I found you. The bullet grazed your skull and maybe knocked you a little loco."

Shorty's head was spinning. He eased himself back on the wagon bed and tried to get things straight. Well, he thought disgustedly, this here's the corker. But it's about what you'd expect, I guess, when a hell-raisin' drover hires on at respectable work. Gets hisself shot right out of the saddle! What I ought to of done was stick with trailin' cows.

But the trail driving days were numbered—Shorty Gibbs had seen that much three years ago, when he first decided to lay over in Hardrow and look for something else. But shot! Who would want to shoot a likable, easygoing, good-time gent like Shorty Gibbs?

Some disturbing answers came readily to mind. It was just possible that he wasn't quite as easygoing and likable as Shorty Gibbs liked to imagine. He had stepped on some tender toes in his day. Short man on a short fuse, they called him. Especially with a few snorts of panther juice warming his belly.

Well, all right, he admitted, he had tramped on a sensitive ego here and there. But there was nobody who actually wanted to *kill* him. There had been times in his reckless past when he'd felt obliged to gun-barrel a few overgrown gents down to his own size—but hell, boys, that didn't mean they'd hunt him down maybe five years later and drygulch him.

Or did it?

There had been that gambler in Wichita—some kind of a row over a leggy saloon girl whose name Shorty couldn't recall off-hand. Or the gunsharp up at Dodge, who, as it turned out, hadn't been as fast as his reputation had led folks to believe. Shorty's bullet had shattered his kneecap. He always walked with a limp after that, Shorty had heard.

"Boy," the old man told him, "you don't look so good. Maybe you better rest a spell."

The old-timer climbed out of the wagon. Shorty

10

could hear the bleating of woollies in the distance. Just what I need in the middle of cow country, he thought sourly—to hook up with a sheepman!

2

The first light of a new morning crept over the prairie. Shorty woke slowly, his insides growling. Dimly, he remembered drinking a gamy broth that the old man had brought to him from time to time, but it had been almost four days since his stomach had known solid food.

The morning sun burned like a gold dollar beyond the puckered end of the wagon sheet. Shorty rose slowly to a shaky crouch. I got to get out of here, he told himself. Got to get back to Hardrow and let folks know what happened. Reckon there'll be a big fuss raised over losin' the mail—but that can't be helped.

"Old man!" he called hoarsely.

The old-timer appeared at the open end of the wagon and loosened the sheet. "The name's Seth Bohannan," he said dryly. "Reckon if you're strong enough to holler you're strong enough to call me by name."

Shorty accepted the rebuke with little grace. "Look, I got to get to Hardrow. You got a horse I could have the borry off?"

"Nope." Bohannan helped him down from the wagon bed and propped him against a wheel. "There's

Mary Ann," he said, nodding toward a toothy, gray-faced mule staked near the wagon. "But she never took much fancy to saddles . . ."

Shorty sighed. No need to worry about saddles—the pinto had run off with his, and he was pretty sure that the old mutton puncher didn't sport one.

The old man grumbled, "I never aimed at a case of trouble when I hauled you to the wagon. You know who it was that parted your hair?"

"You know as much as I do, Bohannan. You right sure you didn't see my mail pouch anywheres?"

The old sheepman snorted impatiently. "I never seen no pouch or no pinto. If Mary Ann's willin', you can have the borry of her to get you to Hardrow." Shorty heard the ring of finality in his words. The old man was beginning to have second thoughts about being a good Samaritan.

Bohannan squinted bleakly at the flock of woollies grazing along a dry run below the wagon. A sheepman in cow country had enough troubles of his own. But there was something about him—a certain grim set to his bewhiskered jaw, maybe—that made Shorty wonder fleetingly if he didn't have something more important than sheep on his mind.

Bohannan set an iron pot off the fire, spooned a meat stew into a battered granite plate and handed it to Shorty. "Here, this'll hold your ribs apart till you get to Hardrow."

Shorty gazed suspiciously at the floating chunks. "What is it, woolly meat?"

Bohannan drew himself up indignantly. "A sheepman don't eat his own. You're more greenhorn than I thought, if you don't know that."

Shorty grunted by way of apology and dug in. The gravy was thick and fiery with chilis and garlic. The meat was on the gamy side, stringy and coarse. "I don't know what kind of cow this is," he said finally, "but she sure wasn't no rich man's pampered pet!"

"Ain't cow," the old sheepman said pitying his guest's ignorance. "She's coyote stew, the way I learned to cook her down in Sonora."

Shorty paled and quickly put the plate aside. "Reckon that's all I can hold." He touched the crown of his head, moving his finger along the scabbed-over furrow in his scalp. For the first time since coming awake in the old man's wagon, Shorty felt strong enough to indulge himself in anger. Yes sir, he thought, a hairsbreadth to the south and he'd of carried off the top of my skull! "I don't reckon you've got a lookin' glass, have you?" he asked.

The old man gave him a blank stare. Shorty told himself it was just as well. Four days in a sheepman's wagon with his scalp laid open, he had a pretty good notion what he looked like. I'm gettin' a funny feelin', he thought, that I just ain't never goin' to be satisfied with myself till I catch up to that fancy shootin' son and . . .

The thought trailed off in anger.

Barebacking on a mule over twenty miles of rolling prairie could be an ordeal under the best of circumstances. Toward mid-morning Shorty's head was pounding, his rump was sore, his dangling legs began to cramp. And the coyote stew rolled uneasily in his belly.

Toward the middle of the afternoon he raised Hardrow, a bleak, dusty, hard-time place at best. A scattering of shanty stores. A few sod houses, most of them abandoned, eroded, sagging on the edge of collapse, some with tall weeds growing out of their dirt roofs. A ranchers' supply town, off the main stage road between Dodge and Tascosa. A colorless oasis on a sun-scorched desert, but a welcome sight to the eyes of Shorty Gibbs.

He reined the mule up beside a brush arbor extension to the livery barn at the edge of town. He eased himself from the animal's bony back and gingerly stamped some feeling into his feet. *Quiet.* . . . The thought crossed his mind idly. Only three horses tied in the street, and not a single rig.

He moved to the door of the barn and called, "Anybody in there?"

The sound of his own voice caused his head to pound. He heard someone coming up from the dark, hay-smelling interior. Murph Hogan, the hulking, red-faced, onion-headed hostler, drew up short, bugging his eyes at Shorty.

"It's *you!*"

"Who'd you think?" Shorty asked impatiently. "Look, I want you to stable this mule while I . . ." He looked closer at the bug-eyed hostler. "What's *wrong* with you?"

"It can't be you," Hogan said dully. "They're all down at Gyp Creek right now with hooks and seines. They're draggin' the whole bottom."

The famous Gibbs fuse was burning short. "What the hell're you talkin' about?"

The hostler gulped. "We was all so sure! Your pinto comin' in with an empty saddle. The mail pouch missin'. Then, findin' your hat, the way we did . . ."

Shorty made a growling sound in his throat. "For the last time, Hogan, tell me what you're blabberin' about!"

Hogan waved his arms in confusion. "You *had* to be dead, Shorty! Ever'thing pointed to it. Ever'thing!"

The beginning of understanding penetrated Shorty's impatience. "They're out draggin' Gyp Creek for *me?* Is that what you're tryin' to say?"

Hogan's bald head bobbed up and down. "Ever'thing was clear as day when we went out and saw where it happened. At first we thought maybe your pinto spooked and throwed you. Then Ab Jergin, he found your hat there on the creek-bank. And the trail of blood. Then we knowed what must of happened."

15

"And just what," Short said acidly, "was that?"

"You was *murdered,* Shorty!" Hogan blustered. "It was all wrote out in the grass where you was shot out of the saddle. The trail of blood led right to the creek—and there was your hat at the edge of the water. What was we supposed to think?"

Shorty felt himself beginning to sag. His legs felt soft. The whang tough muscles of his chest felt like limp buckskin. He didn't know what the citizen of Hardrow was supposed to think. And he didn't much care. Let them think he was murdered, if that's what they wanted.

"Shorty," the hostler blurted, "you *was* shot, wasn't you? You *did* get robbed out of your mail pouch, didn't you?"

"Shot, yes," Shorty said wearily. "Robbed, yes. But you can tell the good citizens they can stop stirrin' up the mud in Gyp Creek. And they can kick the dirt back in my grave. Because old Shorty Gibbs ain't dead yet—not quite."

He pushed away from the barn and aimed himself at the Plug Hat Saloon.

4

Goldie Vale, in her red spool-heel shoes, was half a head taller than Shorty Gibbs. Her hair shone like the polished cuspidors that lined the footrail of the Plug Hat bar. She was dealing herself a hand of blackjack at the end of the bar when Shorty reeled through the door.

"Whiskey," Shorty said hoarsely, resting on the bar.

"Shorty Gibbs!" Her voice was as brassy as her hair. She was genuinely pleased to see Shorty still alive—which, now that Shorty thought about it, was more than he could say for Murph Hogan. "We thought you was . . ."

Shorty gestured wearily. "A sheepman found me and brought me alive on coyote stew." Goldie poured him a drink in a water glass. He downed it, and a soothing heat stirred his sluggish blood, cleared his eyes, sharpened his mind.

Goldie, recovering from the shock of seeing Shorty alive, studied him with a sharper, more calculated gaze. "You talked to anybody since gettin' in?"

"Just to Hogan down at the wagon yard. He told me about the town turnin' out to drag the creek." He tried without much success to grin. "Tell you the truth, I never expected there'd be so much fuss when old Shorty Gibbs cashed in his checks."

She shot him a slitted look that somehow stirred unrest in his mind. "Hogan never told you about the stranger?"

"Not that I recollect."

"The day after your pinto showed up with an empty saddle, a stranger by the name of Courtney landed in Hardrow and started askin' questions about your mail run from Tascosa."

Shorty looked blankly into Goldie Vale's glittery

green eyes. "Where's the stranger now?"

Her face suddenly paled, the reddish freckles across her nose showing up like birdshot. "Since last night, when some of the boys rode over to the blackjacks and cut him down, he's been in boothill."

Shorty stared at her. Outsiders were considered fair game for hurrahing, but lynching was carrying things too far. Even for Hardrow. "I guess there wasn't no trial or anything like that?" he asked with faint hope.

Goldie shrugged. "The circuit judge wasn't expected this way for another month, and the boys was impatient."

Things were moving too fast for Shorty Gibbs. First, some back-shooting gent had nigh busted his head open. And because of that, somehow, a stranger had blundered into Hardrow. A mistake that had cost him a stretched neck. Now, for reasons that were still foggy, the town had turned out to drag Gyp Creek for Shorty's body.

He downed another shot of the fiery liquid. "Now," he said wearily, "let's go back to the startin' line. What was it about this stranger, Courtney, that got folks so worked up that they just *had* to hang him?"

Thoughtfully, Goldie turned up another glass and poured a drink for herself. "Well, this Courtney, for one thing, claimed to be a gambler. But he never turned a card that time he was in Hardrow." She downed her drink. "Come to think of it, he never had much time for cards."

Shorty was getting a curious feeling, an unpleasant

itch that he couldn't quite get at to scratch. "What did he look like?"

She sighted in on Shorty's height of five and a half feet. "Tall," she said. "Six feet, and then some. Kind of a hungry look to him."

A prickling sensation moved over Shorty's scalp. "Black hat?" he asked. "Leather vest? Black boots with butterfly tooling?"

She looked startled. "You know him?"

"Down at Tascosa he had a faro layout. Cleaned me out of everything I had, even that thunderbird concha that I always carried for luck."

Goldie Vale looked suddenly sick. "He won that concha from you gamblin'?"

"I ain't so sure you could call it gamblin', the way he went about it—but he won it." Shorty was disturbed by the taut lines in the saloon girl's face, and by his own growing sense of uneasiness. "What's this all about? What's a Navajo piece of silver got to do with a lynchin'?"

Unsteadily, Goldie refilled both glasses. "It was that concha that clinched things. After they found your horse and all—after they found your hat there by the water, and we all figured you was dead. . . ." She spread her hands in a gesture of helplessness. "After all that, somebody noticed that concha that Courtney was foolin' with. Somebody said that Shorty Gibbs never would of parted with that good luck piece without he was killed first. I guess that's what everybody thought. When they faced him with it, Courtney claimed he'd won it off a mail rider that quartered here in Hardrow. He claimed the only luck it had brought him was bad—so, bein' a gambler and naturally superstitious, he wanted to give it back to the man he'd got it from. That's what he claimed."

Now Shorty experienced a hollow, gutless sensation. Because of a silver concha worth less than a dollar, a man had been hung.

Goldie, meaning well, said, "Drink up, Shorty. You ain't got nothin' to blame yourself for."

"It ain't myself I'm blamin'." He found strength in anger—but how did you go about hating a whole town? "What about the missin' mail pouch?" he asked. "Did anybody think to tie Courtney up with that before they strung him up?"

Goldie smiled—but it wasn't really a smile. "I guess not. When folks get riled they don't think so straight."

"That," Shorty said cuttingly, "is goin' to be a great comfort to Courtney." He wheeled and tramped out of the saloon, leaving his free shot of whiskey on the bar.

CHAPTER TWO

1

The whole business of the lynching had the smell of tragedy about it, but not the accidental or coincidental kind that Shorty had seen so often on the trail. Everything was too orderly—and tragedy was most often a senseless thing. A good man rode off a cut bank on a dark night and died; that was the way it usually worked.

In his rented one-room shack near the wagon yard, Shorty Gibbs went to sleep thinking about the lost mail pouch. What had been in it that was so important that a person would commit murder in order to get his hands on it? Somebody in Hardrow, most likely, because Hardrow was the end of the mail run. Did it have anything to do with the lynching?

It was hours later when he woke to see the bland, broad face of Hoyt Tooms looking down at him. Tooms was the local marshal, the nearest thing to a lawman that Hardrow had to talk about.

Shorty came awake, slowly, a muttony taste still in his mouth, his head still pounding. He gazed blearily at the hulking figure of Tooms, noting that the marshal's clothing was sweat-stained and smeared with mud. "Sorry to disappoint you, Tooms," he said sourly, "but I ain't goin' to drown myself in Gyp

Creek just to ease the conscience of your lynch mob."

"If I was in your boots," Tooms said softly, like a big cat purring, "I'd watch the way I talked. Folks is edgy. We just spent a hard day draggin' the creek, on your account—while you was layin' up in your shack asleep. And the business with that stranger, Courtney. That was on your account too, and folks ain't likely to forget it."

"*My* account?" Shorty swung himself to the edge of his ropestrung bunk. "It's a funny thing." He glared up at the hulking marshal. "Seems like nobody with a name ever done anything bad around here—like drygulching or lynching. It's always 'them' or 'they' or 'folks' or 'somebody.' But nobody you could point a finger at and say, 'that's him.' Don't this strike you kind of funny, Marshal?"

"What happened to the stranger was a accident, Gibbs. The sooner you get that through your head, the better for all of us."

"There you go again. *Us.* Better for *who,* Tooms?"

The marshal's expression didn't change, though his grayish eyes appeared to grow a little cooler. "For you, maybe, Shorty. Nobody's blamin' you exactly—but you can't deny you've put us to considerable trouble."

"I'll apologize for gettin' myself shot," Shorty said bitterly, "when I'm feelin' a little stronger." He lurched up from the bunk, blundered to the washstand and poured a dipper of water over his head. In the scaling looking glass over the washstand he looked at himself for the first time in four days—and it was something of a shock.

His eyes were sunken, his cheeks hollow. Nearly a week's growth of whiskers looked like beard on a dirty-faced corpse.

Ignoring the marshal, Shorty fumbled for soap, lathered his beard and began to shave. Throughout this burst of activity Tooms looked silently in the doorway.

"What do you aim to do about the missing mail pouch?" Shorty asked at last.

The big marshal shrugged. "Nothin' *to* do, except report it to the county sheriff when I see him. It was your job to bring in the mail—I ain't got no jurisdiction outside of Hardrow."

Shorty could see how it was going to be. The fault for everything was going to be his because he had carelessly let himself be bushwhacked. As for the county sheriff—Panhandle counties were bigger than most states. The sheriff probably didn't know there *was* such a place as Hardrow.

Shorty finished shaving in silence. He rinsed his face and cautiously patted his sandy hair over the scabbed furrow. "Where's my hat?" he asked. "Somebody said you found it on Gyp Creek." A man felt naked without a hat—and a contract mail rider couldn't afford to buy a new one every time he got himself shot.

"Over at Goldie's place," Tooms said.

"Has Goldie told you about the stranger you strung up? And that thunderbird concha of mine that he had on him, and how he come to have it?"

Tooms nodded his heavy head.

"I reckon the town's right proud of itself, solvin' the murder that wasn't a murder by stringin' up a man that had nothin' to do with it anyhow. I guess nobody thought to ride to Tascosa and see if there was any truth to his story?"

The marshal gazed narrowly at Shorty, a certain hardness in that bland expression. "You ain't goin' to make trouble, are you, Gibbs?"

Shorty tried to laugh, but it only made his head ache. "All I done was get myself shot and lose a mail pouch. Why would I want to start a ruckus? Of course, if I'd strung up an innocent man, I might feel a little different."

For the first time the marshal came all the way into the shack. The battened walls seemed to bulge as the huge figure filled the room. He placed both hands on the washstand and leaned forward, fixing Shorty with an icicle eye. "Don't get smart with me, Gibbs. About the stranger—it was a bad thing. But nobody's to blame. Feelin' was runnin' high, things got out of control. It could of happened any place." The cat purr had become a velvet snarl.

Shorty gazed flatly at the marshal and wondered if someday he would have to test that old theory about a good little man against a good big one. "You aim to drop the whole thing, is that it? The drygulching, the lynchin', the robbery? You aim to just kick dirt over it and forget it ever happened?"

"It's better that way, for everybody. Courtney's dead. There's no way of changin' that."

"But someplace there's a bushwhacker runnin' loose with my mail pouch. Ain't anybody interested in findin' out who he is?"

"One thing leads to another," the marshal said with steely reasonableness. "Start diggin' for the bandit and you uncover the necktie party. The mail pouch ain't that important—there ain't nobody in Hardrow goin' to make a complaint. Nobody'll ever know you lost the pouch."

"That's right comfortin' to hear," Shorty said with all the sarcasm he could muster.

Tooms shrugged with a hint of weariness. He eased his great hulk through the doorway and was gone. "I'll be damned," Shorty said to the haggard face in the looking glass. "What do you think about that?"

2

Shorty headed for the Ace Cafe and ordered flapjacks, chili, fried steak, and spuds to take the taste of coyote stew out of his mouth. A change of clothing and a sponge bath had rid him of the woolly smell of old Bohannan's hospitality. The sleep had cleared his mind and eased his aching head. With a full belly and a clear eye, things didn't look quite as bad. Maybe he had started to condemn the town without having all the facts.

Old Ben Kramer, the Ace proprietor, sloshed black coffee in front of Shorty, staring at him with a nervous eye.

"No need to be skittish," Shorty told him dryly. "I ain't a ghost—not yet."

"I guess. But it takes a little gettin' used to." Silently, he was asking Shorty Gibbs to take his business someplace else, but Shorty did not listen to silent voices.

"I got some catchin' up to do," he commented, cutting into a piece of dried apple pie. "What can you tell me about that gambler that called hisself Courtney?"

Kramer patted his forehead with a counter rag. "Nothin'. I never seen him."

Shorty's sense of well being began to fade. "That would take a lot of lookin' the other way, considerin' what happened to him."

"Nothin' happened to nobody, far's I'm concerned. I mind my own business." The cafe owner put down the rag, eased down to the far end of the counter and busied himself with a pot of beans.

So this, Shorty thought, is how it's goin' to be. Not findin' my body in Gyp Creek must of been a great disappointment to everybody. But here I am, big as life, to remind the whole town that they strung up an innocent man. He paid for his supper and left.

The street was almost deserted as he headed toward the public corral to see about his pinto. With some surprise Shorty realized that Hardrow was a dying town. It had been on the downgrade ever since the main stage road had bypassed it in favor of Tascosa.

26

I been wastin' my time in this place, he told himself sourly. Two years, and the only things he had to show for his trouble were saddle galls and a sore head.

The wagon yard, like the rest of the town, had that lonesome look about it. Once there had been a string of camp shacks to the south of the barn, but most of them had fallen down or had been knocked down for kindling. Ranchers and cowhands no longer spent their big Saturdays in Hardrow if they had any way of getting somewhere else.

Shorty circled the livery barn, making for the public corral. The pinto was there, fat and contented as a Comanche on allotment day. Murph Hogan came out of the barn wiping his bald head with a bandanna. "You owe me three dollars for boardin' the pinto," the hostler said sullenly. "I'll take the money now."

There was a distinct glitter in Shorty's eye. "Don't we usually settle up at the end of the week?"

"Things is different now. I ain't got room for the pinto in my corral. And while you're at it, take the mule too."

Shorty stared, too puzzled for anger. While he had been sleeping the day away something very interesting had taken place in Hardrow. Suddenly there was no room for two animals in an empty corral. In a town that was dying on its feet a bankrupt hostle turned away business.

With a docility foreign to his nature, Shorty paid up without a fuss. He collected his saddle and rifle. "I've got a funny feelin'," he said thoughtfully, "that if I

27

was to want some feed for these animals, you wouldn't have any to sell. Am I right?"

Hogan squinted. "I got just enough for my regular customers." The hostler was not a perceptive man, but he could see that Shorty's grin was a mask. "I got work to do," he said uneasily, backing away toward the barn.

Shorty staked the horse and mule in the tall Johnson grass behind his shack. Luckily, feed was not yet a critical problem. But he had a hunch that other problems would soon be turning up. Maybe his rented shack wouldn't be for rent any more. Maybe his pinto would go lame and he couldn't hold up his end of the mail contract, and that would be the end of his job. Maybe his credit would be stopped and the various stores in Hardrow would find excuses not to serve him. Queer things could happen, if a man took it in his head to make them happen. A man like Hoyt Tooms, for example.

Once again Shorty became aware of his bare head. In the Panhandle a man usually removed his hat only for funerals and sleeping.

3

The Plug Hat Saloon was doing a good business, considering it was suppertime and most Hardrow citizens were home eating. Shorty counted four cowhands at the bar, and two ranch owners and a Cattlemen's

Association man at one of the tables. The hands and the Association man were wearing guns—there was nothing too unusual about this. Still, more and more townships were passing laws against the wearing of firearms, and it wasn't often that you saw this many guns in one room.

Goldie's night man, George Marquis, was working the lower end of the bar. Shorty gestured to the owner.

Goldie Vale set up bottle and glass, and, without being asked, handed over Shorty's hat. Shorty inspected the head-piece with more than common interest. It was a good, expensive hat—or had been twelve years before. Now it was sweat-rimmed, grease-stained, spotted and streaked from countless unremembered abuses, but it still held its shape in the way that only top grade felt would do. Good as new, almost, Shorty thought bitterly, except for the two holes in the crown and the dark stain that hadn't been there the last time he had looked.

He brushed the hat on his sleeve, creased it so that the bullet holes weren't too noticeable, and set it gently on his tender head. "Thanks," he grunted.

Goldie shrugged. "Now you've got everything you had when you landed in Hardrow. Don't you think it's about time you looked for better diggin's?"

Shorty looked at her in faint surprise. "You, too, Goldie? Looks like everybody else is tryin' to nudge me out of town, but I thought me and you was pals."

Goldie looked at him as if the bullet had done permanent damage to his brain. "Why do you think I bother with you? Maybe you ain't noticed, but you ain't exactly the most popular gent that ever rode into Hardrow. A businesswoman in these parts could do a lot better than bein' pals with Shorty Gibbs."

Shorty poured himself a shot from the bottle. "I knowed the town had gone sour—but it ain't that bad yet, is it?"

"All I know is what I see. Over there at the table sets the second biggest rancher in this end of Texas, Emery Straiter. Next to him sets the third biggest rancher, Paul Maston. The long, drawed-out gent drinkin' with them, is Sam Milo, top inspector for the Cattlemen's Association. You know how long it's been since any one of them has showed his face in Hardrow?"

Shorty grunted and downed his drink.

"More than a year," Goldie said, as if she were making an important point. "Can you guess what they wanted to know, every one of them, as soon as they come through the door?"

Shorty shook his head.

"They wanted to know if I'd seen Shorty Gibbs. Like they couldn't believe you wasn't actually dead."

"They ain't the only ones to be disappointed."

Goldie's grin was like a flashing knife. "So you *have* started to feel it. Don't it mean anything to you when somebody nearly kills you, and then everybody you know tries to crowd you out of town?"

"Sure, it means Hardrow's a town with a mighty guilty conscience."

Goldie snorted. "Shorty, you're a fool."

"I guess," he agreed. "Or I never would of settled here in the first place. But now that I'm here, I don't aim to be crowded out, or bluffed out, or scared out. If they want me out they'll have to carry me." His grin was wide but a little strained. "Anyhow, like you said, Straiter and Maston ain't really the top dogs around here. When John English and his Spur bunch starts gunnin' for me, maybe then I'll start to worry."

Goldie shook her head sadly. "What kind of flowers do you favor? In case I take a notion to plant some on your grave."

She turned to take care of another customer who had just pushed through the swinging doors. Shorty watched her with narrowed eyes and had to admit that she was a handsome woman—but he didn't care much for her sense of humor. The new customer stood at the bar between the group of cowhands and Shorty. He was obviously a working hand himself, but a first class one. He had the lean, tough look of a full-time saddleman. His clothing was plain and dusty, but of top quality. Shorty noted the plain black boots, old and scuffed now, but handmade, and would have cost a top hand half a year's pay when new. A foreman, Shorty decided. At least the top hand of some cowman's regular crew. He wore a common wood-handled .45 on his right hip. Shorty, without a pistol on his belt, was beginning to feel undressed.

Goldie Vale set out glass and bottle, collected the newcomer's silver and returned to Shorty. "You recognize the gent in the black boots?"

He shook his head.

Goldie flashed one of her edged grins. "Name of Nate Corry."

Now Shorty had him pegged, and he came suddenly erect, scowling. Corry was John English's foreman— top dog of the Panhandle cowmen. "Maybe," he said to the red-haired saloon owner, "I'm a more important man than I realized."

From out of the south a chill breeze drifted into the Plug Hat Saloon and flowed across the back of Shorty Gibbs' neck. Goldie said worriedly, "I wish I knowed what was goin' on. Shorty, you just ain't important enough to bother cowfolks like John English." She shook her head, copper ringlets swinging at her shoulders. "I ain't seen this kind of thing since the Carrizo sheepman tried to move down to the Panhandle."

"When was that?"

"Four years ago. Before you landed here. But there ain't no sheep trouble now. The only mutton puncher I've heard about is the old geezer that fed you coyote stew and . . ."

But Shorty Gibbs was gone. Unpredictable as prairie wind, he had simply jammed his hat down on his injured head and tramped out.

4

The smell of woodsmoke and the simmering slum in the iron pot made Shorty's stomach roll. He reined up a short distance from the wagon and called, "Old man, you up there? It's me, Shorty Gibbs."

A high, pale moon shone down on the colorless grass and white sheeted wagon. Shorty held the lead rope over his head. "I brought your mule home, old man."

Seth Bohannan, a shadow moving out of darker shadow, stepped away from the wagon and came toward his visitor. In his right arm he cradled an ancient, long-barreled rifle. He lowered it, almost grudgingly.

"It ain't that I'm not proud to get Mary Ann back," he said slowly, "but don't it strike you a mite queer, bringin' a mule home this time of night?"

"There's somethin' I wanted to talk about." Holding to Southwest rules of etiquette, he did not dismount until the old man gestured for him to do so.

"I can't say who shot you," Bohannan said, taking the lead rope, "if that's what you want to know."

They walked up the slope to the wagon, leading the animals. The old man stopped beside his fire and tied the animals to a wagon wheel. Shorty circled the simmering pot, hunkered on the windward side and methodically began to build a smoke. "Was you down in these parts four years ago, durin' the sheep trouble?"

The old man hunkered on the opposite side of the fire. "Nope. Them was Mex herders."

"You mind tellin' me what you're doin' down here in cow country?"

33

Bohannan considered the question. "The flock goes where the grass is. I follow the flock."

"Even if it takes you into dangerous territory?"

The old man studied him over the glowing coals of the fire. "What did you come here for, besides to bring Mary Ann?"

Shorty told him what little he knew concerning the strange actions of the town—and it was little enough. "It ain't that I hate the notion of gettin' out of Hardrow," he explained, "but I can't quite swallow the idea of gettin' *run* out. You know what I mean?"

The old man lifted his head, solemn and proud. "I know."

"Well, that's how it is. First the wagon yard turns down my business, then the town marshal starts to ride me like he was breakin' in a new saddle. Next, the town starts to fill up with important cowmen, and they all want to know about Shorty Gibbs. But the thing that brought me here is somethin' a saloon girl let drop. She said she hadn't seen the cow clans gather this way since the sheep war. You couldn't be gettin' yourself mixed up in a war, could you, Bohannan?"

The old man wagged his head. "Just me and a few dozen sheep. We ain't worth the bother."

"Just the same, you're flirtin' with trouble. I've seen cowfolks that would shoot a sheepman just to see him bleed."

A strange stiffness settled on Bohannan's features. "So have I," he said in a voice without tone or timbre. He stared past and through Shorty Gibbs, seeing things in the night that no man should ever have to see. "So," he said again, "have I. That's how they killed my boy just to see him bleed. That's how they killed Ramon. . . ."

Old Bohannan got to his feet and without so much as a nod in Shorty's direction, tramped off into the night.

By the time Shorty got back to Hardrow the best part of the night was gone. The pinto plodded into the dark, deserted town. A smoky haze hung over the shabby collection of frame shanties. The prairie wind, on a rare whim, was still. Shorty leaned over the pinto's neck, scowling, his head cocked. That haze—almost like a fog, but you didn't see fog on the High Plains—heaved sluggishly on some upper wind current, permitting pale moonlight to filter down on Hardrow.

It was perfectly normal, Shorty told himself, for a town to be quiet only two, three hours before sunup. But this was a little too quiet. Instinctively, he moved his right hand to the stock of his saddle rifle. The Winchester was already half out of the boot when the dark figure moved into the street, in front of the livery barn.

Tooms. No other man in Hardrow would loom so big in an empty street.

Shorty unsheathed the Winchester and levered a cartridge into the chamber in one smooth motion. Tooms did not move but merely waited, standing hipshot, almost in an attitude of boredom. "You ain't goin' to need that rifle," the marshal said. "Not now, anyhow."

Shorty nudged the pinto forward, cautiously, sniffing the air, houndlike. The haze wasn't a haze after all. It was smoke.

He eased the rifle back into the boot. "Ain't it a little late for the town law to be prowlin' the streets?"

"Maybe. But you keep pretty queer hours yourself."

Shorty ignored the unasked question of where he had been. He sniffed again at the acrid air. "What's been burnin'?"

"One of the shacks back of the bar." The big lawman regarded him thoughtfully. "Your shack, Shorty."

Shorty jerked erect in the saddle. But with unusual control he made himself swallow the information and digest it before speaking. "It ain't like I ever claimed you for a sidekick, Tooms," he said coldly, "but I never figured you for a house burner, either."

The marshal moved his heavy shoulders. "When I get enough of you, Shorty, I won't burn you out. There's other ways."

"Would you like to try some of them, Marshal? Right now?" His admirable control was slipping. Anger rushed in, hot and demanding. He threw himself out of the saddle, grabbing the Winchester on the way down. "Go ahead, Marshal!" He realized that he was yelling. The sound of his voice rolled over the silent town like a shot from a brass Napoleon. "I invite you, Tooms! Try to get rid of me, any way that suits you."

The huge lawman heaved a ponderous sigh. "Some other time, Gibbs. Not tonight."

"What's the matter, Tooms? You waitin' to get a clean shot at my back?"

The marshal's grayish eyes seemed to glisten in the pale light. But his voice was unruffled, soft and smooth as honey. A big cat purring. "That ain't quite my style, Shorty. I waited up to give you a message from Goldie Vale—she's left the back door of the saloon unlocked. You can bed down there, if you want to."

Shorty's grip on the Winchester relaxed. He knew that he had made a fool of himself. "All right," he said ungraciously. "You delivered the message." He reholstered the Winchester and led the pinto to what was left of his shack.

It wasn't much—a blackened doorframe leaning crookedly against a piece of a wall. A heap of charred rawhide lumber, still smoking. A few coals glowing red in the darkness.

Tooms had trailed him silently to the edge of the rubble. "We ain't sure how it happened. Not long after you pulled out a cowhand come in the Plug Hat and said a shack was burnin'. There wasn't nothin' anybody could do—the closest fire barrel was clear around in front of the livery barn."

"Right thoughtful of somebody," Shorty said bitterly, "furnishin' entertainment for all our important visitors." He glared at the marshal. "So you just stood and watched it burn!"

"For a little while," Tooms said blandly. "Then I went back to the saloon and had a beer." Before

Shorty could explode, the big lawman backtracked softly, melting away in the night.

The darkness bore down on Shorty. He felt hollow. These past few days had sapped his strength. He stood for a long while staring blindly at the smoldering rubble.

"After thirty-two years," he thought aloud, "all I've got to show in the way of property is a painted horse, a wore-out ridin' rig and a twelve-year-old rifle." Add the clothes that he wore on his back. The rest—what little there had been—buried beneath the charred remains of the shack.

"But they ain't goin' to run me out," he said to the smoking ruins. "And they ain't goin' to burn me out, or scare me out. They ain't goin' to get rid of me any way at all, unless they kill me."

Now that it had been said out loud, he felt a little better. He grinned wolfishly at the darkness. "And killin' me, boys, is apt to take some doin'!"

CHAPTER THREE

1

He staked the pinto in a patch of mullein and Johnson grass behind the Plug Hat Saloon, then tried the back door. It was unlocked, and Shorty entered cautiously, somehow feeling like a burglar.

An unpleasant thought crossed his mind. What if this was all Tooms' doing? What if the marshal, for reasons of his own, had arranged to have that door unlocked? And what if he was to appear suddenly, gun drawn and cocked, a conscientious lawman anxious to do his duty? Wasn't that the way Tooms would tell it later? "Took him for a burglar," as he pointed to the body of Shorty Gibbs, cold and stiff, stretched out on the saloon floor.

Shorty shrugged disgustedly. His imagination was fighting the bit. Tooms had his faults, but outright murder probably wasn't one of them.

He struck a match and lit a reflector lamp. Goldie had made him a bed on the pool table near the end of the bar. He scouted the saloon carefully for no particular reason, except that he had never been in a saloon like this before, all by himself, in the dead of night.

He returned to the rear of the building and barred the back door. I've seen softer mattresses, he thought, thumping the rock-solid pool table. He blew out the lamp, shucked his spurred boots and stretched full length on the bed of slate. Being short sometimes had its advantages.

He lay in darkness, wide-eyed, unable to sleep. Carefully, he hazed his thoughts away from house burners and bushwhackers—he'd never get any rest thinking about *them*. Queer about old Bohannan, though. A sheepman striking out by himself in cow country. Queer, and maybe suicidal as well. Shorty wished vaguely that he knew of some way of helping the old mutton puncher—but there wasn't any. Bohannan was his own man. And Shorty had troubles of his own.

His thoughts turned to Goldie Vale. Who else in Hardrow would have the gall to house Shorty Gibbs when it seemed that everybody else was trying to prod him out of town? In her own brassy way, she was a lot of woman. Plenty of gall and gumption. And a full share of looks.

But there were times when Goldie looked at him in a certain way, sizing him up, kind of, like he was the last runty stud in a horse sale and she needed one more animal to make a team. But Goldie wasn't his type. He told himself this every day or so, just to keep things straight in his own mind.

His thoughts floated and kept returning to one thing that he couldn't understand, and maybe it was the key to everything. What had been in that mail pouch?

The kind of mail that usually came to Hardrow you wouldn't cross the street to claim. As Hardrow didn't

40

sport a bank, there wasn't much chance that he had been transporting a big sum of money without his knowing it.

Suddenly he was off the pool table, pacing the saloon floor in his bare feet. Automatically, he twisted a smoke and lit it. Why would somebody want to kill a mail rider for a handful of "back home" letters, a few mail order catalogues, and the usual assortment of harness and patent medicine advertising?

He helped himself to a generous shot of Goldie Vale's whiskey and spoke to the dark mirror behind the bar. "I don't know. But it *has* to be the mail pouch."

Through the window he watched false dawn lighting the far horizon. He returned to the pool table.

2

George Marquis, general swamper and part-time bar-keep for the Plug Hat, was sweeping the previous day's litter on the front door when Shorty came awake. According to the ornate banjo clock over the back bar it was almost ten o'clock.

He hauled himself off the table, stiff of back and shoulders. He gazed blearily about the saloon. "How long you been here?" he asked Marquis.

"Maybe half a hour. Miss Goldie said not to rouse you." George was a big, good-natured man who, in Shorty's opinion wasn't too bright.

He stamped into his boots, walked stiffly out of the saloon and washed his face and finger combed his hair at the public pump at the end of the street. His scalp wound itched, which meant, he hoped, that it was healing.

Goldie Vale had left her living quarters several hours earlier than usual and was boiling coffee on a heating stove when Shorty returned to the saloon. She looked at him in that certain way that always made him uneasy. "I see you made yourself at home with my whiskey," she told him.

"What do you do, put a mark on the bottle every time a drink is poured?" He adjusted his bullet punctured hat on his tender head. "If you don't want your liquor drunk, don't let ex-trail drivers sleep in your place of business."

She grinned. "It's your pretty disposition—no wonder ever'body loves Shorty Gibbs."

"Ever'body," he said sourly, "but the citizens of Hardrow, and some very influential cowmen and their crews, and a bushwhacker and a house burner."

She laughed—a bright, ringing sound, like kicking a heavy dog chain off the back of a wagon. "Have some coffee."

He grunted and took a chair. Goldie poured inky coffee into heavy mugs that she kept for serving Tom and Jerrys at Christmastime. "Well," she said, "I wouldn't say you're the handsomest gent I ever laid eyes on, but you look some better than you did yesterday."

He ignored the pleasantry. "I don't reckon it would do any good to ask how my shack caught fire, would it?"

She shrugged. "First thing anybody knowed, it was burnin'. There's other shacks."

"Not for Shorty Gibbs, I got a hunch." He stared at her for a moment. She had looks, all right, but so did a steel gaffed fighting cock. Soft and gentle and quiet she wasn't. But when you asked her a question you could reasonably expect a straight answer. "Goldie, do you know what any of this is about? Why, all of a sudden, Shorty Gibbs gets on Hardrow's tar-and-feather list?"

"Town's a little touchy. Guilty conscience, I guess, after the hangin'. I don't feel so good about it myself." She tried her coffee and grimaced. "Maybe folks just don't like bein' reminded of what they done—and that's what you do, just by bein' here."

Shorty glared out at the dusty street.

"Maybe," Goldie said, with a sidelong look from those green eyes, "it wouldn't be such a bad notion if you left Hardrow for a spell. If you're shy on cash money, I could let you have . . ."

"No, thanks," he snarled. Starting the day on bitter coffee and anger. "Funny thing about gettin' bush-whacked. It makes me wonder why somebody was so set on killin' me. I'm beginnin' to think he wanted that mail pouch, but I won't be real happy until I know why. Anyhow, I've got the mail run to make—I reckon I've still got the job . . ."

Goldie was shaking her head. "Straiter and Maston and English sent word to the contractors that the mail service in these parts wasn't satisfactory. A new rider has been put on in your place."

Shorty came out of his chair. "They can't do that! I got a contract!"

"Good as long as you give satisfactory service." Goldie shrugged characteristically. Take things as they come and don't drop your guard, was Goldie Vale's philosophy.

Shorty checked his temper. Straiter, Maston, and English. The three big cowmen working together could do almost anything that came into their heads. But John English, the biggest of the bunch— somehow, it didn't seem reasonable for a man like English to concern himself with such things.

Goldie said, casually, "English and some of his Spur hands rode into town last night."

Shorty whistled softly.

Goldie shot him a guarded look. "You sure you wouldn't like to see some other part of the country?"

"It ain't travel I need, it's answers to some bothersome questions."

3

The three cowmen and the Association man, Sam Silo, were eating an early dinner in the Ace Cafe when Shorty came in. Shorty blandly ignored Ben Kramer's

44

look of distress, tramped back to the big table and, uninvited, helped himself to a chair.

For a long, silent moment they stared at him—the Association man with anger, Straiter with faint but cold interest, Maston with icy detachment. John English gazed at the unwelcome visitor as if he had been a particularly unpleasant type of insect, something to be batted away and smashed beneath his bootheel.

Sam Milo was the first to speak. He leaned forward menacingly. "You wasn't invited here, Gibbs. Move on somewheres else."

Shorty grinned his insolence at the cowmen. "I'm invitin' myself. You gents have dealt yourselves into my business. So you'll just have to get used to lookin' at my face."

"Not for long . . ." Milo started. A glance from English stopped him. He sat back, faintly flushed, as if he had just been reined down with a Spanish bit.

"It's just as well that you joined us, Gibbs," English said. "Sooner or later we'd have to meet. Folks say you're a stubborn, short-tempered man. So's an old wrinklehorn cow just out of the brush—stubborn and short tempered. You know what happens to old wrinklehorns. They wind up in a slaughterhouse." He cut a piece of steak and chewed thoughtfully.

Shorty's gaze moved from face to face. All three ranchers were speaking with English's voice—that much was clear. Even to men like Straiter and Maston, the word of John English was law. Paul Maston, a gaunt gray-bearded man in his late fifties, sat in aloof silence. Straiter, tall, sun dried and toughened, gazed at Shorty with unfocused anger. English, older than the others, also bigger, tougher and more ruthless, put down his knife and fork.

Shorty said evenly, "I understand you boys got together yesterday and shot my mail ridin' job out from under me."

Sam Milo grinned, but it was English again who spoke for the group. "That's about what happened. But it wasn't much of a job anyway. We decided you could do better for yourself somewheres else."

"Especially," Sam Milo added impulsively, "since your shack burned down and you ain't got a place to stay."

He was silenced by three looks as hard as bullets. The Association man cowered back in his chair and was not heard from again.

"Why'd you do it?" Shorty asked with icy control.

English shrugged. "You are a disturbin' influence to the country. We'd rather you went someplace else."

Shorty shook his head. "Not many days ago I was shot out of the saddle and had my mail pouch robbed. I won't be happy till I know why."

The gazes of the three ranchers met for an instant. John English drew a leather money purse from his coat pocket and shoved it across the table to Shorty. "Maybe," the cowman said icily, "this will help you forget that business on Gyp Creek."

Shorty took the purse, scowling, and unfastened the metal clasp. What he saw startled him. He glanced quickly at the three faces. "There must be two, three hundred dollars here!"

"Five hundred," English informed him blandly. "In double eagles, Gibbs. Gold. Good anywhere you want to spend it."

Straiter spoke for the first time. "Anywhere but Texas." Three heads nodded agreement.

Shorty was stunned. He had never owned five hundred dollars in his life. Just cinch down his saddle and travel, and these double-eagles were his! He shoved the purse back to English. "It ain't that I couldn't use the money. But I'd rather have some answers."

Expressions of surprise and anger flitted across the faces of the cowmen. "Gibbs," Paul Maston hissed, "you're even more of a fool than I thought!"

"And in this country," Straiter reminded him, "the life of a fool can be a short one."

Something happened to Shorty Gibbs' sun-browned face. Around the mouth deep, defiant lines appeared. His eyes narrowed and seem to glitter as he looked from face to face. Then he kicked back his chair and stalked out of the cafe.

Goldie Vale groaned when Shorty told her about the purse. "Five hundred in gold! Maston was right. You *are* a fool."

"It could of been a thousand; I'd still have to know who tried to kill me. I'd have to know why cowfolks get mixed up in the doin's of a mail rider. And I'd have to know why a gambler by the name of Courtney got hisself hung so sudden."

Goldie regarded him with a mixture of impatience and concern. "If you're just set on bein' bull-headed, I can't stop you. But if it was me, I'd be practical and take the money."

Shorty, on his way out of the saloon, paused at the door and grinned tightly. "You happen to notice how many customers you've had since you opened up this mornin'? None. You think it might be on account of the company you keep? Folks you let sleep on your pool table? That what you call bein' practical?"

Shorty paused beneath the Plug Hat's plank awning, watching the ranchers leave the Ace Cafe. Two riders entered the street at the wagon yard end and headed toward the cowmen—one of them Shorty recognized as Nate Corry, the Spur foreman. The other was a husky young man, fair haired, handsome in his own arrogant way. His expensive riding rig was gaudy with Mex and Navajo silver. The pearl handle of his revolver gleamed in the sun like a gold tooth.

Goldie Vale came up behind Shorty, standing in the saloon doorway. She looked at the two riders and groaned, "Vance English!"

Shorty glanced back with a sour grin. "Big as life, ain't he? The light of the old man's eye, they say."

Goldie Vale, who never claimed to be a lady, snorted in an unladylike manner. Vance and the foreman had reined up in front of the three ranchers, and the young Spur heir appeared to be holding an urgent discussion with his father. John English was shaking his head, his old face a stone mask.

The young man's face flushed with anger. Obviously he had asked for something and had been denied. "Now there's somethin' a-body don't see every day," Goldie said dryly. "John English shakin' his head to that spoiled pup of his."

"He's a little late," Shorty said, wondering what the family gabfest was all about and wishing they'd talk louder. "He ought to of started sayin' 'no' about twenty years ago."

Goldie mused to herself. "Wonder what brought him back to Hardrow? I kind of figured it would be a spell before he plagued this town again."

Shorty squinted, only half-listening. "Why would an English shy away from Hardrow?"

"After what happened? You said it yourself—that stranger, Courtney, did get strung up kind of sudden. And Vance English was right in the van of things that night. Spoutin' lynch talk louder'n anybody."

Shorty exhaled in surprise. "I didn't know Vance was in town that night."

"You don't stay in one place long enough for anybody to tell you anything."

Across the street young English was getting hotter all the time, and his father was still shaking his head with grim stubbornness. Angrily, Vance reined his animal away from the group and headed back toward the wagon yard at a full gallop. Old John English turned to his foreman and motioned him to go with his son.

After a moment Shorty pushed back through the

swinging doors. "Tell me some more about the hangin'."

Goldie made a sound of disgust, went behind the bar and poured a drink for herself. "Vance and the English foreman, Nate Corry, rode in about sundown that day. Saloon business was good—there was a lot of talk about the killin'—your killin'—and some of the boys was gettin' kind of hot. First thing I knowed, somebody had mentioned breakin' Courtney out of jail. I can't say who. But Vance was soon talkin' it louder than anybody."

She downed her drink and set the bottle out of sight. "I wouldn't listen to it. I told them to change the subject or I'd send the whole bunch packin'." She sighed. "Maybe someday I'll learn to keep my mouth shut. Vance flared up, like he always does when ever'thing don't go to suit him. Said they'd just move to the Great Western and he'd buy drinks all around. That's the last I seen of them. And it's all I know."

The Great Western Saloon was a slap-up affair on the windward side of the public corral, specializing in doctored whiskey and faro. The owner was Phil Sublet, a small, slightly soiled but dapper man with a reputation that he didn't like to talk about.

Sublet regarded his customer with suspicion. "You're off your track, ain't you, Shorty. Seems like you take your business to the Plug Hat, as the usual thing."

Shorty came into the drab saloon, his eyes slitted, watchful, as he might enter a bear cave. "I just need some information," he said, as Sublet was reaching for a bottle.

The Great Western owner leaned across the bar, smiling faintly. "About what?"

"The mob that strung up the stranger, Courtney. They left the Plug Hat that night and come here. Who was leadin' them?"

"There wasn't nobody leadin' them. And it wasn't a mob—just a few of the boys havin' some drinks."

"Who was buyin'?"

Phil Sublet brushed his neatly trimmed mustache. "I don't recollect."

"Who was the first to mention necktie party?"

The barkeep shrugged. "Never heard anything about a necktie party. Like I said, they was just a few of the boys havin' a drink."

"Was Vance English with them?"

Sublet patted his forehead with a soiled linen handkerchief. "I don't recollect."

Shorty, with no sign of warning, leaned forward, grabbed the front of Sublet's vest and almost jerked him over the bar. "Phil," he said softly, "I ain't talkin' just to hear my head rattle. Somebody tried to drygulch me, in case you ain't heard, and I'm the kind to take a thing like that serious."

He twisted on the vest, knotting it at the barkeep's throat. "I've got this fool notion," he said in a tone of extreme reasonableness, "that the bushwhackin' and the lynchin' kind of went together. So you see it's somethin' more than idle gab—I've got a personal interest in the matter, you might say."

The saloon owner flapped his arms helplessly, his face turned red, his eyes bulged. Sublet was an inch taller than Shorty, and as heavy, but he had never spent eighteen hours a day in the saddle trailing two thousand head of nervous cattle.

Shorty tightened his grip. "You beginnin' to recollect now?" he asked quietly.

Sublet gulped air and rubbed his throat. "Sure he was," he said shaken. "Anybody could of told you that."

It occurred to Shorty that the saloon had become noticeably darker. He let the barkeep go and turned toward the door. Hoyt Tooms was standing in the opening, smiling grimly, his huge figure blocking out most of the light.

"You do keep busy, don't you?" the marshal said dryly.

"Look here, Tooms!" Sublet sputtered. "I was right here in my own place of business when he come in and . . ."

"I know," Tooms said wearily. "Shorty, maybe it's time for me and you to talk."

"What kind of law are you!" Shorty flared. "Sublet was right here that night, seen every man in that mob, heard everything they said. Why don't you question him?"

"I have," Tooms said with an air of great patience. "Now I want to talk to you." He stepped back from the doorway.

Curious as to what this was all about, Shorty let Sublet go and moved into the street with Tooms. He stared up at that big, bland face. "Come to think of it, what was you doin' while that mob was haulin' Courtney out of jail? Does the marshal take his orders from that spoiled pup of John English's?"

Tooms flushed. Suddenly that bland face was no longer bland, it was hot and angry. His voice was still soft, but not gentle soft—soft as the whisper of a flying bullet. "If you was a little closer . . . ."

"Closer to your size?" Shorty glared up at him. "Don't let my height and weight stop you, if you got it in your head to start somethin'."

The marshal clinched a ham-sized fist convulsively. Then, with a mighty effort, he pulled himself in. He said, in a strange and constricted voice, "I was in my office when they took Courtney. They got the drop on me—there wasn't anything I could do."

"There wasn't anything you could do," Shorty repeated sarcastically. "You wasn't blind, was you? You could see who was in the mob."

"They had coffee sacks over their heads." He stared angrily down on Shorty. "Anybody could of told you that, if you'd thought to ask. But you never think, do you? You just grab folks by the throat and start to shakin'."

"Maybe. But that don't change the fact that Courtney was your responsibility, and you let them hang him. Don't tell me a man you've knowed most of your life can put a coffee sack over his head and

53

you wouldn't recognize him." He pulled up for a moment, scowling. "That's it, ain't it?" he went on thoughtfully. "You did recognize them. But they was all pals of yours, or big brand cowmen, so you let them have their way."

Tooms had turned pale. In his eyes was a faintly glazed cast that might have been mistaken for pain. "You listen," he said harshly, "because I don't aim to say this but once. Maybe I did recognize some of them. And maybe they was pals of mine. But for all anybody knowed, Courtney was a murderer, and you was the one he murdered. What was I goin' to do— lose a prisoner, or kill my friends? What would you of done?"

Shorty exhaled through clinched teeth. Finally he had the truth—part of it. But he wasn't fool enough to think that Tooms would repeat it in front of another witness. Shorty turned his thoughts back to Vance English—Vance had his faults, but would he stir up a lynching just for the sport of the thing? For no better reason than the pleasure of watching a man kick at the end of a rope?

4

It was nothing but a hunch, and not much of a hunch at that, but it was all he had to go on. In a burst of action Shorty got the pinto saddled and left Hardrow in a wake of reddish dust.

That scene between Vance English and his father was still nagging in the back of Shorty's mind. What could be important enough to cause the youth to bare his fangs at the old man? It might prove interesting to trail Vance and Nate Corry and see what the pup was up to.

For several minutes he held the pinto to a gallop, keeping to a rutted wagon track that Vance and Corry had taken out of Hardrow. There was no sign of the riders. No man-horse specks along the ridges, no revealing streamers of dust. Maybe Vance and the foreman had cut cross-country and headed back for Spur headquarters.

Shorty didn't believe it. Vance had fogged it out of Hardrow too full of purpose.

Suddenly, down at the bottom of a gentle slope, he saw the two riders calmly sitting their animals beside the wagon track. A buckboard with a plodding roan between the shafts was coming toward them, coming from the southwest, the direction of Tascosa.

It was obvious to Shorty that Vance and the foreman had ridden from town for the special reason of meeting this buckboard. Their attention was on the rig and nothing else. Shorty squinted against the sun. The distance between himself and the buckboard was too great to tell much about the person in it, but not too great to see that it was a woman.

He nudged the pinto forward along the dusty road. There was something about the figure of Vance English, rock-still, purposeful, that started a ripple of uneasiness up Shorty's spine.

Then, stretching casually, Vance reached for his saddle rifle. He had the rifle half out of its leather sheath when the foreman glimpsed Shorty riding toward them from the opposite direction. Nate spoke to his young boss, and must have spoken sharply. Vance froze. Then he glanced quickly over his shoulder and shoved the weapon back in place.

What did it mean? Shorty knew what it looked like, but he couldn't make himself believe that even a head-strong whelp like Vance English would set out to drygulch a woman.

He covered the distance between himself and the two Spur men at the gallop. Vance was smiling crookedly, anger glittering in his eyes. Nate Corry nodded curtly, his expression as blank as a side of meat on a butcher's block. Shorty reined up beside him.

"Well," Vance drawled, "if it ain't the short man with the long string of hard luck. Between me and you, Nate," he said to his foreman, "I got a feelin' the string's goin' to get longer and harder. And pretty god-damn soon at that."

"I lost somethin' all right," Shorty said. "My job, my mail pouch, the house I lived in, and most of my plunder!"

Vance grinned unpleasantly, "That's a sad story, little man. But I'm afraid me and Nate can't help you. We was headed back to the Spur."

"Takin' a mighty long way around, wasn't you?"

"Little man, an English rides any way he feels like."

"Call me 'little man' once more," Shorty told him coldly, "and I can point out one English that'll have to buy hisself a new set of front teeth."

Vance's grin was almost an expression of pain. "Sorry, Mister Gibbs, but me and Nate ain't got time to set here and jaw. Come on," he said to his foreman, "the company here's beginnin' to gall me."

They must have rehearsed it—the thought flashed through Shorty's mind when he saw that he was about to get himself caught in the jaws of their trap. Nate's horse, suddenly skitterish, had sidled out of the slot between Vance and Shorty. "Easy, boy," the foreman said quietly. "Easy there." The animal tossed its head, cross stepping in a small half circle. Almost too late Shorty recognized the commotion for what it was— expert horsemanship on the part of the foreman.

Vance was watching closely, his upper lip curled, part grin, part sneer. Suddenly Shorty found himself caught between the two Spur men. The trap was closing. Maybe it had already closed. Vance, with that unpleasant sneering grin, was directly in front of Shorty, grabbing for his pearl-handled .45. Shorty cursed himself for a fool. All he had was the Winchester, and not nearly enough time to use it.

He kicked spur steel into his animal's ribs. The startled pinto lunged forward, crashing head on into Vance's animal, all but unseating the rider. For a few seconds the two men clawed and slashed at each other.

"Shoot!" Vance yelled hoarsely to his foreman.

57

"Goddamn you, shoot!"

But, for the foreman, it wasn't as simple as all that. The horses kicking and twisting in a frenzy created a reddish whirlwind of dust. The two riders, each struggling to unseat the other, made a single target. "Shoot!" Vance cried again. But Nate, expert shot that he was, realistically calculated his chances on hitting the right man in all the confusion. He didn't like the odds.

He decided to let Vance, for once, settle his own dust. The foreman didn't look as if he cared much, one way or the other, if both of them had to buy new teeth.

Shorty had clamped a steel-like grip on the front of young English's vest; with his other hand he lashed out blindly. Vance, feeling himself falling, kicked himself free of the stirrups. He struck the ground with a curse in a mushroom of dust. Before he could get to his feet Shorty had also freed himself of the pinto and was diving on top of him.

A short distance away, on the spring seat of the buckboard, the woman sat frozen, watching the violent proceedings in a kind of terrified fascination.

CHAPTER FOUR

1

Vance English, for all his flashiness, was no milk-fed veal. He was young, strong, arrogant. Shorty's head rang from a hammerlike blow beside the left ear. Rolling, cursing, flailing at each other in the boiling dust, Vance grabbed again for his revolver. Shorty, with a snarl, clubbed it out of his hand. I don't much like your style, boy! I just don't like drygulchers, if you want the truth of the matter!

A bullet-like fist in the midsection sent the young Spur heir stumbling back. Shorty lunged, this time bloodying the youth's mouth. Don't let my size fool you too much! He thought hotly. A mighty little bullet can do a heap of damage! Still and all, he reasoned, there ain't no sense tusslin' here in the dirt when there's an easier way . . .

He grabbed Vance by his collar, then let go so suddenly that the young cowman stumbled and almost fell. Shorty swooped down with his right hand and grabbed that gleaming pearl-handled Peacemaker out of the dust.

"That's—all!" he said hoarsely. Indelicately, he rammed the muzzle of the .45 into Vance's gut. He maneuvered the rancher so that he stood as a shield between Shorty and the Spur foreman. "You too!" he snarled at Nate Corry. "Drop your pistol. Then we'll see just where we stand."

Corry gazed with momentary blandness at Vance's mask of rage. Then, with an invisible shrug, he dropped his weapon. "You're callin' the shots, Gibbs—for now."

Vance was livid. "Goddamn you, Nate! Wait till the old man hears about this!"

Nate Corry ignored him. "What do you aim to do now, Gibbs? Shoot Vance and me, in front of a witness? Or do you aim to shoot her too?"

"That's what you two was aimin' to do, wasn't it?"

The foreman's expression of innocence was too elaborate. "You're talkin' loco, Shorty. Why'd me and Vance want to do a thing like that?"

". . . I don't know," Shorty had to admit. "I'll let the marshal back at Hardrow ask you. And maybe the county sheriff."

"Now I know you're loco," Nate said in a broad, pitying tone. "Folks would laugh you right out of the Panhandle if you started to claim a thing like that."

It was the truth. And Shorty, in the cool, reasoning part of his mind, knew it. Even Vance began to see it. His arrogance returned.

"What about that, little man . . . ?" But the words trailed off as Shorty withdrew the muzzle from his midsection and took thoughtful aim at the center of Vance's face.

"I wouldn't do it, Shorty," Corry said coolly.

"I guess not. Anybody that takes his orders from John English's pup."

Bullets might have had some effect on Corry, but not words. He shrugged indifferently. But Vance's eyes were glittery. He was seeing Shorty dead, seeing him stretched out stiff and cold on some coffinmaker's slab.

They had reached an impasse. The woman in the buckboard, all but ignored by the three men, stared at the scene before her in disbelief. After a moment of silence, Corry said in his lazy way, "Looks like it's up to you, Shorty. Take us in and turn us over to Tooms, or let us go. What's it goin' to be?"

He had to let them go. There wasn't a person in Hardrow who would believe that he had happened along just in time to stop Corry and Vance English from bushwhacking a lone woman.

"Well . . . ?" Nate Corry asked.

Shorty nodded stiffly, as though the effort pained him. "Round up the horses."

Corry flushed the animals and hazed them back to the road. Vance grinned unpleasantly in Shorty's face.

"I'll take my gun now, if you don't mind."

"I mind," Shorty told him bluntly.

The grin vanished. All of Vance's ugliness was about to boil over again, but in the background Corry was making soothing sounds. He was silently saying, let it go. They'd settle up later with Shorty Gibbs. At a time and place of their own choosing.

Shorty kept them covered with Vance's fancy .45 as

the young cowman got mounted. "This has been a big day for you, little man," Vance told him viciously. "You better enjoy what's left of it—it might be the last one you'll see."

They wheeled their animals and rode away from the road. Methodically, Shorty scooped up Corry's pistol and shoved it in his waistband. Then he tramped over to the pinto and dropped Vance's fancy killing piece into the saddle pocket. Only then did he turn to the stunned woman in the buckboard.

"Ma'am," he said wearily, "womenfolks just ain't got any business travelin' the prairie by theirselves. Don't you *know* that?"

She stared at him for what must have been several seconds. He saw her hands begin to tremble. Nervously, she wrapped the lines and held her hands together in her lap. She was a colorless woman, very prim in a limp sort of way. There was something about her that suggested sickness, though she looked healthy enough at first glance. It flashed through Shorty's mind that he had seen her somewhere before.

Her pale lips moved several times before she made a sound. "What . . . was that all about? Who were those men?"

Shorty squinted. "You didn't know them? Never seen them before?"

She shook her head. "Never."

"English. That name mean anything to you?"

"I've heard it, of course."

"That's all?"

She nodded.

"Corry?"

She looked blank. "I don't know any Corry."

Shorty believed her. She wouldn't be very good at lying. "Ma'am," he said bluntly, because he wanted to know, "you got any notion why them two gents would want to kill you?"

The question startled her. "Kill!"

"That's how it looked to me." He could still see Vance reaching for the saddle gun—there had been real purpose in that action.

The woman shook her head violently, "Oh no, you must be mistaken!"

He saw that he had frightened her. "Maybe," he said. But that wasn't much help.

She clasped and unclasped her hands. "I can't believe it . . . Why would someone want to . . ."

"I was hopin' you could tell me," Shorty said.

"I don't understand." Shaking her head. There was worry and fear in her voice—and Shorty thought he could hear the first raspy edge of panic. "I just don't understand. Unless . . ." She shot a quick, suspicious glance at her inquisitor. "Who are you? If what you say is true, how do I know I can trust you?"

"The name's Gibbs," he said patiently. "I ride . . . I *used* to ride mail between Hardrow and Tascosa."

"That's the name Ralph mentioned when . . ."

Shorty felt himself tense. His scalp prickled. "Ralph who?"

"My husband," she said worriedly, still clasping and

unclasping her hands. "Ralph Courtney."

Oh Lord, Shorty thought dully, staring at the pinched and worried face of the dead gambler's widow.

2

With ice in his gut he thought, somebody's got to tell her. But not me. Let somebody in Hardrow do it. Tooms, maybe. Or one of the bunch that broke Courtney out of jail and strung him up. Let one of them explain to the gambler's widow that it had all been a mistake.

"You know my husband," she said. It was almost an accusation.

"No ma'am, not exactly," Shorty hedged. "We got into a game of cards over in Tascosa. That's the only time I ever seen him." But that wasn't quite true. He had seen Courtney once before that, driving a hack down the main street of that cowtown—and this woman had been beside him. Shorty hadn't paid much attention to her then, but now he recognized that pallid, worried face. Even then, before anything had ever happened to Courtney, she had been worried.

"But," she was saying, "you're the same man Ralph took that luck piece from. That's the reason he gave for coming to Hardrow."

"Gave?" Shorty pounced on the word. "You mean it wasn't his real reason?"

Something in his eyes or in his voice added to her growing concern. "Something's happened to my husband. What is it, Mr. Gibbs?"

Shorty told himself there was no sense putting it off; he might as well tell her.

"Mrs. Courtney . . ." He couldn't do it. Not like this, out in the middle of the prairie with not even another woman around to comfort her. He tied the pinto to the back of the buckboard. "There's a man in Hardrow—marshal by the name of Tooms. Maybe you better talk to him."

He saw her shiver, as though Death had brushed her with a dark wing. Shorty climbed to the seat and rustled the line. They rode in silence, and not once did the woman voice the question that towered between them. She already knew the answer.

It was dark when they got to Hardrow. The street was all but deserted. No sign of Vance or Nate. No sign of the cow outfits. Just a nice, quiet little town where nothin' ever happens, Shorty thought bitterly.

The woman had pulled into a shell of silence. There was a brittle look about her, as though a word or a sudden sidelong glance might shatter her. Shorty stopped the roan in front of the Plug Hat. "Mrs. Courtney . . ."

He could have been invisible. She turned and looked straight through him.

"I ain't sure where the marshal's at. I better ask in the saloon." She nodded without hearing. "You'll be all right here in the rig," he told her. "I won't be gone but a minute." She nodded again, blankly.

Shorty cursed himself for a spineless snake. I ought to of told her, he thought. What's the sense of stringin' it out, keepin' her guessin'? Only, judging by her looks, she wasn't guessing. She knew.

It was the slack hour for saloons. Goldie Vale was dealing Sol at the bar. A pair of town loafers lounged at one of the tables and George Marquis, the roustabout, idly twisted the chuck-a-luck cage. Shorty stepped into the flickering lamplight and said, "Anybody seen Tooms?"

Goldie glanced up. "He passed the door not long ago." Then Tooms, as though he had been signaled, appeared in the doorway.

"Ain't that your pinto tied to the buckboard out there?" He moved to the bar with surprising lightness and stood for a moment, gazing flatly down at Shorty Gibbs. "Who's the woman?"

"Well, now," Shorty said bitingly, "if you'll just think back a little maybe you can recollect a dude by the name of Courtney that went and got hisself lynched a few nights back in this peace-lovin' little town of yours."

"Don't get smart with me, Gibbs," Tooms rumbled.

"Oh I ain't bein' smart, Marshal. You wanted to know who the woman is, and I'm tellin' you. She's Courtney's widow."

Tooms paled visibly. Goldie Vale made a strangely un-saloon girl sound. "That poor woman!"

"Except," Shorty said cruelly, "she don't exactly

know she's a widow yet. Not for sure. I figured," he told Tooms, "the honor of tellin' her ought to be yours, seein' as how you was the one that let the boys take him out of the jail that night."

The marshal grew red in the face and looked as though he might choke. Then he wheeled and lurched toward the door. Goldie Vale glared at Shorty. "One day—and it don't figure to be long off—you're goin' to snipe at Tooms once too often . . ." But the angry thought trailed off. "That poor woman," she said again, in what was almost a whisper.

3

"Ma'am," the big marshal was saying, "if you could tell us somethin' about your husband . . ."

She looked at him with a strange lack of emotion. "Ralph . . . My husband's dead, isn't he?"

The words were without tone. But emotion was not absent; it was only delayed by shock. Shorty and Goldie moved into the street with Tooms. The two loafers were in the saloon doorway peering curiously at the dark figures.

In reflected lamplight, the marshal's face looked drawn and pale, and suddenly Shorty wasn't so proud of the way he had broken the news to Tooms. He wasn't so proud of the way he had handled any of this.

"Ralph," that distant voice was saying, "is dead, isn't he, Marshal?"

Tooms shifted in great discomfort. "I hate to say it, ma'am, but he is."

She stared through the marshal as she had stared through Shorty. "I think I've known it all day; I just didn't want to admit it. I knew it even before those men stopped me . . ."

"What men?" Tooms asked sharply.

"I'll tell you about it later," Shorty said. "Ma'am, you mentioned something about that luck piece of mine. Is that what brought your husband to Hardrow?"

She smiled, a strangely disturbing expression based in pain. "Ralph said it was as good a reason as any."

"Why did he need a reason?" Tooms asked.

She looked at them and answered obliquely, and Shorty thought, the shock's beginnin' to wear off. "Ralph was no gambler, not really. He only pretended to be one. It was part of his job. He said all gamblers were superstitious. He said he could claim the silver-piece—the one he won from Mr. Gibbs—was bad luck for him. That way nobody would think it queer if he rode all the way to Hardrow to give it back to its original owner. Ralph said that's the kind of thing a real gambler would do."

"If your husband wasn't a gambler," Tooms pressed, "what was he?" He too sensed that the moment of apparent calm was nearly over.

Mrs. Courtney looked surprised. "Why, Ralph is a . . ." She caught her mistake. "Ralph was a detective for the Cattlemen's Association."

Shorty and Tooms crossed startled looks. "Was he investigatin' somethin' in Hardrow?" the marshal asked quickly.

"I . . . don't know." The blankness was beginning to leave her eyes. "Ralph never told me about his work for the Association. But he had already written a report and mailed it."

Shorty came instantly alert. "Mailed it when? Who to?"

She shook her head. "I don't know." She closed her eyes tightly in hopeless concentration. "Is it important?" she asked at last.

"Yes ma'am," Tooms said gravely.

"Would it help you find . . . ? Find the man who killed Ralph?"

"Yes ma'am, it might."

She knotted her fists and ground her knuckles against her eyes in an effort to remember. "It was on the day," she said, "that my husband won the silver piece from Mr. Gibbs. That was the day he mailed the report."

Shorty shot a glance at Tooms. "It was in my mail pouch! That's why I was drygulched—somebody wanted to get his hands on that report!"

Tooms ignored him. "Ma'am, can you tell us who the report was sent to?"

She shook her head. "I don't know. There were sometimes two reports; one going to the Association members requesting the investigation, and one going to Association headquarters."

She continued to shake her head from side to side, and finally she began to sob.

"Give me a hand!" Goldie said sharply to the two men. "Get her up to my place."

It was not what Shorty and Tooms would have liked for a "proper lady," as Mrs. Courtney obviously was; the quarters of a saloon girl. But it was the best they were likely to get—they didn't fool themselves on that score. If anybody was to play the good Samaritan it would have to be Goldie. The "decent" women of Hardrow were too busy soothing the guilty consciences of their menfolk.

As they helped Mrs. Courtney down from the buckboard Shorty saw what it was about her that had made him think of sickrooms or invalids. There was something wrong with her back that caused her to stand bent over in a perpetual crouch. She twisted her head painfully, looking up at Shorty as her feet touched the ground.

She looks like a proud woman, Shorty thought silently. She must hate it, havin' to look up to people all the time.

It was an hour later. Mrs. Courtney had been given a dose of Goldie Vale's private drinking whiskey in a hot toddy and was resting in Goldie's quarters over the saloon. Shorty and Tooms were talking in the town's one cell calaboose which, in a pinch, served as an office for Hoyt Tooms. The two men hunched forward on the rope bunk, a tallow candle sputtering on the floor in front of them. Shorty had just given an account of his meeting with Vance and Nate Corry.

"You're loco," Tooms said bluntly. "The son of John English settin' out to drygulch a lone woman! And takin' along the old man's foreman as a witness! Do you expect me to believe a story like that!"

"I was hopin' you would," Shorty said with an edge of a snarl. "Because it's the truth."

The marshal wagged his head stubbornly. "Did you see Vance take a shot at her?"

"I told you he never got that far along with his scheme. I happened along and changed things."

"Did you see Vance threaten her?" Tooms pressed.

"I saw him reach for his saddle gun."

"He pulled his saddle gun out of the scabbard and pointed it at Mrs. Courtney as she came toward him in the buckboard?"

Shorty's anger flared. "You know he never pulled the gun; I already told you."

"But he reached for it," Tooms said dryly. "How do you know he wasn't just brushin' off some dust. And even if he was reachin' for it, how do you know he aimed to threaten Mrs. Courtney with it?"

"Not threaten," Shorty grated. "Kill." But this was getting him nowhere. Grudgingly, he pulled in his temper and confessed, "I know it ain't much of a story. And there ain't nobody that would back me up on it. Not even the woman knows what kind of danger she was in."

The bunk groaned as Tooms shifted and searched for makings. He built a smoke in silence. "How can you be so sure you're right about this?"

"What it boils down to, I guess," Shorty admitted, "is a hunch. The way Vance looked. Mean, and kind of scared, too. There was kill written all over him." He had half-expected Tooms to laugh, and if he had, Shorty had planned to hit him with the first heavy object he could lay a hand on.

But Tooms didn't laugh. He smoked silently until only a dead ash was in his fingers. "What," he asked finally, "do you expect me to do?"

"For one thing, you can find out about the second copy of that report. It was supposed to go to Association headquarters, according to Mrs. Courtney. If the Association has it, maybe it will tell us what's at the bottom of our trouble. But I don't think they'll have it."

Tooms shot him a guarded look. "Why?"

"Maybe I wasn't the only mail rider that got hisself waylaid that day."

The marshal sighed. "How come Courtney rustled up that watery excuse to come to Hardrow? The report was in the mail. The case was finished, as far as he was concerned."

"Maybe Courtney had some second thoughts on the subject. Or maybe he just decided to go over the ground once more, in person."

"Seems to me," the marshal rumbled, "there's a lot of maybes in this scheme of yours. On the other hand, it don't hardly stand to reason that you could be wrong *all* the time . . ." He grinned faintly—or maybe it was

72

a trick of the flickering candlelight. "Anyhow, I guess no harm'll be done if I go to Tascosa and ask a few questions."

Shorty sat in surprised silence. He hadn't expected his story to be believed—that was too much to hope for. What he had expected was a long, hot argument, getting him nowhere and probably ending in violence. Now he felt a little better. Maybe Tooms was smarter than he had thought.

Both men turned quick eyes toward the open cell door. Someone was coming toward them from the direction of the saloon.

The brass-haired saloonkeeper stepped into the open doorway and gazed with weary humor at the two men, one huge and sometimes maddeningly deliberate; the other small, impatient, all steel spring and rawhide.

"She's sleepin'," Goldie said finally, her sardonic air vanishing.

"Did she talk any more?" Tooms asked.

"A little. She kept askin' about the two men that stopped her on the road. And she mentioned another rider she met earlier. She asked him about the condition of the road to Hardrow."

"Did she know him?"

Goldie shook her head. "No, but she asked the rider about her husband. So that horsebacker knew all about *her*. Don't it seem funny that he claimed he'd never heard of Courtney—a hand on the payroll of a local cowman?"

Shorty came up from the bunk. "What cowman?"

"She described the brand on the rider's animal. Bar-Circle, she called it. That would be the rowel brand of John English's Spur, wouldn't it?"

Shorty turned a sharp gaze on the marshal. Until now he hadn't been able to explain how Vance and Nate Corry had known that Courtney's widow had been traveling that road at that particular time. One of Vance's own Spur riders had told him.

Tooms shoved himself up with a grunt. "I'll start to Tascosa in the mornin'," he told Shorty. "Might be a good idea if you make yourself scarce till I get back."

"And who'll look out for Mrs. Courtney?"

Goldie shrugged, as though there had never been any question about it. "I will."

4

For once Shorty took Tooms' advice—as the marshal rode with the dawn for Tascosa, Shorty struck once more toward Gyp Creek where the whole thing had started.

The old sheepman had moved his wagon over a rise and into another valley. The new camp was located on a green bend of the creek; the woollies dotted the bright slopes like lint balls on green felt. Just why he had returned to Seth Bohannan's camp, Shorty was unable to explain to his own satisfaction. But the sheepman hated cowmen, and Shorty was beginning to appreciate the old man's point of view.

Between the wagon and the creek he saw the mule grazing in the tall grass, and from somewhere beyond the mule there came a sound that he thought at first was a sheep. Maybe a lamb that had strayed from the main flock.

Then he heard the sound again. It was no lamb.

Scowling, Shorty got down from the saddle and tied the pinto to a wagon wheel.

As if he had suddenly sprouted out of the ground, Seth Bohannan rose up from behind the creekbank and stood before him, frowning. "What you after, Gibbs?"

Annoyance showed in Shorty's expression. "I ain't after anything. I just got to thinkin' about your trouble with cowmen—and my own trouble, the way it's shapin' up, is with cowmen too. So I got to figurin' . . ."

"Nobody asked you to my camp." The old man gestured with his long-barrel rifle. "Now get your pinto and let me be."

Shorty was more puzzled than angered by the old man's hostility. "Look," he said slowly, "I didn't aim to butt in on anything. But I thought I heard . . ."

The old man glared. "You never heard a thing!"

Shorty, in his abrupt way, tramped through the tall weeds directly at Bohannan. The old man swore and threw down on him with the rifle.

"Stop right there, Gibbs!"

Shorty advanced until the rifle muzzle was almost against his chest. Then he paused and grinned. "See there, old man, you wasn't goin' to shoot anybody."

Suddenly he forgot what had been in his mind. He stared, not at the old man or the rifle, but at a second man. Now Shorty knew where the sound had come from.

The man was staked out hand and foot with rawhide thongs, spread-eagled on the reddish clay near the edge of the stream. He stared wildly at Shorty, working his mouth and uttering the same sound over and over. The word he was trying to say was "water."

CHAPTER FIVE

1

Old Bohannan was watching him sharply. "This ain't none of your business, boy."

"Looks like I dealt myself in anyhow, don't it?" Shorty scrambled down the side of the clay bank. The old sheepman grasped his rifle and studied Shorty's back, undecided for the moment whether to give in to anger or resignation.

His jaw set grimly, Bohannan half raised the rifle as Shorty knelt beside the spread-eagled man and began working at the rawhide thongs. *Fool!* those burning eyes were saying. *Well, I warned you!*

Shorty glanced up at him. "Well?" he demanded hotly. "If you aim to kill me, there ain't much sense puttin' it off, is there?"

Bohannan lowered the rifle—but it cost him something. Suddenly he looked like what he was, an old man on the edge of desperation.

The fact that Shorty had for a moment stared into the cold eyes of sudden death and forced it back a step was no cause for elation. Bohannan could still change his mind about using that rifle. "You got a knife, old man?" Shorty asked bitingly. "I can't work this rawhide with my bare hands."

Tough as briar-root, Bohannan glared at him and did

not move. Shorty snorted impatiently, jerked off his hat and filled it with gyppy water from the creek. The spread-eagled man strained forward, his eyes bulging. He made that sound again and it grated on Shorty's nerves like lava grit.

"Here." He dribbled a little of the water in the man's mouth, and Shorty saw now that he was quite young, not much more than a boy. Cowhand, from the look of his dress. A badly frightened and thoroughly dehydrated cowhand. His lips were cracked, his tongue swollen, his throat parched. Shorty half-turned and snarled over his shoulder. "How long've you kept this man without water?"

Apparently Bohannan had decided against using the rifle. He climbed down the clay bank and gazed bleakly at the two of them. "Not so long," he said, answering Shorty's question. "Since yesterday sometime. Reckon he was already dried out when he come on my camp."

Questions demanding answers crowded Shorty's mind, but for the moment he let them wait. He dribbled more water on the man's cracked lips. "That's enough," he said. "This here's gyp water. She'll give you a big cramp in the gut if you take too much."

The youth was beyond tasting the bitter minerals. He gulped the water and worked his mouth, croaking, begging for more. "A knife," Shorty snapped at Bohannan. "This man'll be lucky if the circulation ain't already stopped in his hands and feet, the way you got him lashed down."

Bohannan gave no sign that he had heard. He gazed at them with growing bleakness and indifference. This, the look said, had been an experiment that hadn't quite worked out. It simply meant that he had tried it on the wrong man—this time.

Angrily, Shorty scooped more water in his bullet-punctured hat and soaked the strips of rawhide. He circled the cowhand, kicking and tugging at the stakes. At last the water softened the rawhide enough to work the loops off the youth's hands and feet. "Water!" he croaked again. His throat was not so dry now, his tongue not quite so thick.

Shorty gave him a little more. "Any feelin' in your feet?"

The shaken young man nodded. "A little. Mister, I don't know where you come from, but I sure am proud you showed up. I thought I was done for!"

"Rub your hands together," Shorty told him. "Get the blood to movin'. Now what's this all about?"

"Mister, I was hopin' you could tell *me*." The hand was beginning to know anger, and that was good. "I never seen this old buzzard before in my life. I ain't been ridin' for Mr. English but for two weeks. Anyhow, my line pardner says to me yesterday he heard about a mutton puncher down in these parts. So I figured I'd take a look. In case my boss was interested."

Shorty interrupted. "You ride for John English?"

"That's right. Name's Bert Stoufer. Could I have a little more of that water?"

"Better not. There's sweet water up at the wagon, but you have to take it easy."

"I sure was dried out!" Bert Stoufer stared angrily at Bohannan. "What's wrong with that old gaffer! Is he loco?"

Shorty shrugged.

"Well . . ." The young man went on. "Like I said, I rode down this way to see about the mutton puncher, when this old ground owl jumped out of a weed patch and throwed down on me with that crazy rifle of his. Next thing I knowed, here I was, stretched out to cure, like a green hide. Ridin' in the sun all day, I was already cotton-mouthed when he stuck that cannon in my face."

"Why did he stake you out like that? He must of said somethin'."

"Oh he said somethin', all right. Same thing, over and over. Who killed Ramon?"

Shorty squinted. "What?"

"That's all he'd say. Who killed Ramon? He'd go off for a spell, and then he'd come back and say it again. Who killed Ramon?" He looked again at Bohannan, not so much in anger this time. "I guess he's loco, all right. It's the only way to figure it."

"Ramon was his boy," Shorty said wearily. "He died not long back. I guess the old man ain't got over it yet."

Bert Stoufer stared, not knowing what to say. "Things like that happen, I guess," he managed grudgingly. "But I've had enough of *that* old buzzard!"

"Will you do me a favor, Bert?"

"Mister, I wouldn't of lasted till sundown if you hadn't come by. You name it."

"What's happened here—I want it kept quiet. I'll head the old man away from Spur range, but I'd just as soon that John English didn't know about this for a spell."

The cowhand scowled. He worked for English, which gave the rancher first claim on anything he knew that might affect the outfit. On the other hand there was a good chance that he owed Shorty Gibbs his life. "Well," he said finally, "it ain't likely I'll be seein' anybody soon. Like as not I won't see the boss for the rest of the summer unless I make a special trip to headquarters."

Shorty grinned. "You able to walk?"

"I can make it to the wagon all right, if there's some water up there that ain't gyp."

2

Shorty found Stoufer's horse, a gray gelding with the Spur "rowel" on its hip, grazing in the deep grama below the old man's wagon. He fed the cowhand out of Bohannan's meager stores, and held him back from the water keg to keep him from foundering. Finally, when the day was nearly over, he got the young man pointed toward his line camp, some the worse for wear but grateful enough to be alive.

Seth Bohannan had watched it all in stony silence. At last, when Stoufer was only a distant dot on the prairie, he said, "If you think that cowhand'll keep his mouth shut, you're a bigger fool than I figured."

"I don't think we better talk about fools," Shorty told him coldly. "If John English finds out about this—and he will, sooner or later—you won't last to see the next day. You, your mule, your sheep, you'll all be out there rottin' in the sun. Sheepherders don't spread-eagle cowmen and leave them to die; not in this country. Don't you know that?"

"I only know," Bohannan said flatly, "that Ramon is dead. My boy is dead. And a cowman killed him."

Shorty groaned. "You think that kid of a cowhand did it?"

"Maybe not. But maybe he knows who the killer is. Maybe I would know by this time, if it hadn't been for you."

This harmless-looking old man, Shorty thought bleakly, would have let that kid die. Not easy to believe, but true. The price of hate—the old man's kind of hate—came high.

Bohannan hunkered down by the fire that Shorty had built. "Go away," he said quietly. "What I do I do for my boy."

"Even murder?"

"A hundred murders, if that's what it takes. But I will find the man that killed Ramon. Killed him for pleasure. Because he tended sheep. Is that any reason to kill a man?" He held that thought at arm's length while staring at Shorty. "Why'd you come here anyhow?"

"I tried to tell you, before I knowed about that Spur rider, but you wasn't in much notion to listen."

Now the old man remembered. "I don't need your help, Gibbs. And I don't want it. And you better not plan on gettin' any more help out of me."

"What do you aim to do?" Shorty asked bitingly. "Ramble around the prairie waylayin' cowhands?"

Bohannan shrugged. "Somebody knows about Ramon. Maybe lots of folks. A thing like murder won't stay quiet."

For a time Shorty was silent. It wasn't the Southwest way to put personal questions to a man, not even one that had saved your life, but it was time to make an exception. He said slowly, "You want to tell me about your boy? I've been in these parts a spell—was the killin' somethin' I'd of heard about?"

Those old eyes smoldered. "It was four months back. We was over to the west, between here and Tascosa. I was down in a creek bottom huntin' squirrels, a mile or more from the wagon where Ramon was. It was still early in the day when the two horsebackers come to the wagon. I heard the shootin'—but the horsebackers was gone by the time I got there. Ramon was there. Three bullets in his chest. Shot twice, just for the sport of the thing, after the first one had killed him. Some of the sheep was gutshot and bleating. The wagon was fired but I got there in time to put it out. They would of shot Mary Ann, I guess, but I had her

83

staked out in a dry wash where they failed to find her."

He told it in a steely monotone, not looking at Shorty. "I reckon," Bohannan continued flatly, "it ain't never an easy thing to lose a boy, but to have a boy like Ramon shot for sport . . ." He looked at Shorty. "But I ain't loco, if that's what you're thinkin'." He rose to his feet and seemed to tower over the flickering fire. "It's just that I aim to find the man that killed Ramon. One way or the other. No matter what it takes. No matter who might be standin' in the way. That goes for you, Gibbs, like everybody else." He hesitated, then added in a tone even colder than before. "So don't get in my way again."

Shorty couldn't blame the old man for feeling the way he did, but he was only going to get himself killed playing loose and easy with big-time cowmen. "I'm sorry about the boy, but . . ."

But what? Suicidal as it was, at least the old man had a plan. And Shorty had nothing to offer in its place.

For a moment the ironlike cast of the old man's features seemed to soften. "I got nothin' against you, Gibbs. I don't want to have to kill you. Will you stay out of my way?"

Shorty answered with another question. "Will you do me a favor?"

Bohannan shrugged.

"Move your sheep away from here. There's a few nesters down south that ain't too crazy about cowmen. They'll put you up on their land for a few days—not that it'll stop the likes of John English and his friends from tryin' to kill you, but . . ."

Bohannan was shaking his head. "I got a man to find. Nobody's goin' to kill me before I find him."

Shorty was silent for a time. Then, abruptly changing directions, "Recollect the gambler that got hisself hung over at Hardrow?"

The old man grunted.

"Name of Courtney. That mean anything to you?"

Bohannan squinted. "What's a dude gambler got to do with Ramon?"

"Nothin', most likely. But Courtney was a detective workin' for the Cattlemen's Association . . . It's beginnin' to look like he was doin' undercover work hereabouts, unbeknownst to the local cowmen." Did the old man's eyes come suddenly into focus or was it a trick of firelight? "That might mean he was diggin' into the doin's of some of the local Association members."

The old man moved so that the light no longer touched his face. "That might be, but it ain't any interest to me."

"You sure?" Shorty asked. "This here's strong cow country. Everybody depends on the ranchers; even the nesters would starve out if they didn't have the cowmen to sell their crops to. So it don't stand to reason that any Panhandle man in his right mind would go complainin' to the Association about their own members. But that's what somebody must of done, if Courtney was actually workin' undercover."

"A cow organization listenin' to a sheepman? That would be a day to mark time by!"

"If it was murder they might listen."

"To a sheepman?" Bohannan asked again.

". . . No, I guess not." No matter how he tried, Shorty couldn't see the Association listening to anything a one-mule mutton puncher might say. He grunted with weariness, got to his feet and took the pinto's reins.

"Watch yourself, old man. You'll have the English outfit after your hide, if that young hand decides to talk."

"Thanks to you," Bohannan said bitingly.

Shorty climbed to the saddle. "If I can do anything . . ."

The old man stood there, deaf and blind as an oak post to all that he didn't want to see or hear.

3

Shorty was sleeping in the whiskey storeroom of the Plug Hat Saloon when Tooms found him and jarred him awake. He sat up on his blanket pallet. "What did you find in Tascosa?"

"About Courtney, not much. Him and his wife was there maybe a month. Claimed to be a gambler but didn't spend much time at the tables."

"He caught and cleaned *me*," Shorty said. "He spent enough time at the tables for *that*."

"That was no accident. Seems like Courtney specialized in cowhands and other folks from these parts. Around Hardrow, I mean."

"Then he *was* investigatin' somebody around here."

"That's how she looks."

"Does sheep figure in it anywheres?"

The marshal shook his head. "Don't look like it."

"Did you find out about the report?"

Tooms' smile was as thin as a Mexican razor. "I talked to the postmaster. Sure enough, there was two reports. Two thick envelopes, anyhow—the postmaster remembered them because of the weight. One went in your mail pouch but he don't remember who it was addressed to. The other one started to Fort Worth on the stage."

Shorty sucked in a deep breath. "Started?"

"The coach was waylaid," Tooms said with the same thin smile. "Half a day out of Tascosa."

Shorty shoved himself to his feet. "That's right interestin'." Bushwhacking a mail rider and robbing a stage coach on the same day. That took some doing. One man couldn't have done it; it would have taken two at least. He clinched his fist. "I sure wish that postmaster could remember who that report I was carryin' was addressed to."

Tooms regarded him thoughtfully. "Goldie says you was out of pocket last night."

He replied with a question. "You ever hear of a kid called Ramon? Ramon Bohannan?"

The marshal frowned. "Nope."

"His old man's a mutton puncher. The kid was killed

not long back somewheres between here and Tascosa, maybe by cowmen."

Tooms was shaking his head, slowly. "I never heard about it. What's it got to do with last night?"

"The old man's the one that saved my hide when I got myself drygulched. I was out to his camp. I had a crazy notion . . ." He still wasn't sure how far Tooms could be trusted. A marshal's wages was barely enough to keep a man going; but a rancher like John English, if he had need of a lawman, could afford to pay handsomely. "You still aim to do nothin' about Vance English for tryin' to drygulch Courtney's widow?"

"Nothin' I can do," the marshal said. "It would be your word against the Englishs'. How far do you reckon I'd get with that?"

Shorty glared, turned on his heel and tramped out of the storeroom.

Goldie Vale was lounging against the bar of the deserted saloon. "How's the widow doin'?" Shorty asked.

Goldie seemed vaguely worried. "She wants to talk to you."

Shorty showed faint surprise. "What about?"

"She didn't say. I left her sleepin' this mornin' to open the saloon. When I took her somethin' to eat at dinnertime she asked to see you."

"Well . . ." He felt in a way responsible for her, and the least he could do was talk to her. "All right." He mounted the stairs to Goldie's rooms.

The door opened immediately. Almost as though she

88

had been waiting nearby for his knock. "Please . . . come in, Mr. Gibbs." She stepped back quickly and Shorty could see that she was unstrung and nervous, which was to be expected. What, he wondered, do you say to the widow of a man who had been lynched in the town where you live?

"Mr. Gibbs, please . . ." She gestured distractedly at a chair, staring up at him from her awkward and painful crouch. "Miss Vale was very kind to permit me . . ." She left another sentence unfinished, made meaningless gestures with her hands and looked as though she might break down at any minute.

Shorty tugged at his hat. "Ma'am, I got a pretty good notion how you must feel about . . . I mean, considerin' the way the boys broke in the jail and . . ." He was only making things worse, as he could see from the stricken look on her face.

"Mr. Gibbs, would you do me a very great favor?"

Shorty nodded gravely. "Yes ma'am, if I can. I aim to do everything I can to track down the leader of that lynch mob." She paled suddenly and Shorty knew that once again he had said something wrong, though he couldn't think what it was. It seemed reasonable to assume that the most important thing in her mind right now would be catching the man responsible for her husband's death.

Apparently he was wrong. "No," she said in a tone that was more weary than grieved, more bitter than outraged. "I'm sorry," she started, "to cause you so much trouble."

"It ain't any trouble," he said solemnly. "None that I wouldn't of found for myself anyhow, sooner or later."

She looked at him with red-rimmed eyes. All her tears, Shorty thought, had already been shed. There was a certain dryness about her that fairly rustled. "What good would it do?" she asked flatly. "Would it bring Ralph back? Would it pay the debts I've been left with? Would it buy my food and lodging and see me safely through the years ahead?" She shook her head grimly. "No, Mr. Gibbs, it would only cause more grief. I've been thinking about it, most of the morning and some of the night. And I don't want to go on with it. I just want to get away from this mean place and forget . . ."

Shorty stared. "You don't want your husband's killer caught? Is that what you're sayin'?"

"I'm saying it would serve no purpose. I don't want vengeance—I'm not that kind of woman." Her nervous gaze flitted over his head and to the side but never met his straight-on. "I only want to leave here, and forget."

"It ain't quite that simple," Shorty said with a certain grimness of his own. "There's been murder done, and it's the marshal's job to work on it. And the county sheriff's, when he's located. Think about it, Mrs. Courtney. To walk away from it would mean lettin' your husband's killer go scot-free. You don't want that, do you?"

At last her flitting, worried eyes did meet his for the

barest tick of a second, and what he saw there was a bleakness that left him chilled. "Frankly, I don't care about the killer now—he can't do any more hurt to me. I only wanted to ask you, Mr. Gibbs, to let the matter be. Just . . . let it be!"

Suddenly she turned from him, and a grave-like chill seemed to settle in the small room. He reached slowly for the door latch, hoping that the interview was over, only wanting to get out and clear his head in the open air.

"Mr. Gibbs . . ."

Shorty cleared his throat. "Yes ma'am."

"Like as not," she said harshly, "Ralph brought his trouble on himself. That's the way he was. Never satisfied to let matters rest. My husband forced and plagued folks beyond endurance. He said that's what made a good detective. And I said, more than once, that it would one day get him killed. And now it has. So let it be."

Shorty worked with his battered hat. "I can't do it, ma'am. I'm in too deep myself."

"I don't have much money," she said quietly, "but I could pay you some . . ."

Shorty stared at her with a kind of bewildered, unfocused anger. "No ma'am. Right now money ain't the thing I need most."

4

Goldie Vale watched with female curiosity as he came down the plank stairway to the saloon. "From the look of your face, it must have been a right important set-to."

"Interestin', anyhow," he said with bite.

"Mrs. Courtney's all right?"

"All right?" He poured himself a drink from a bottle on the bar. "Losin' husbands to lynch mobs could be a regular thing with her, the way she's takin' it." But that wasn't quite true. The red-rimmed eyes hadn't been faked, nor the gray grief on her face. He snorted in frustration. "Maybe I just don't understand women. You seen Tooms?"

"He followed you out of the storeroom and headed for the street." Puzzlement and the beginning of worry showed in her eyes. "What happened up there, anyway?"

But Shorty Gibbs, in perfect character, had wheeled and was gone.

CHAPTER SIX

1

Sam Milo, the Association man, was picking his teeth in front of the Ace Cafe when Shorty came out of the saloon. So the cowmen were back in town, Shorty thought to himself. Where Milo was, English and Straiter and Maston were usually close behind. Sure enough, the three ranchers filed out of the cafe and stood for a moment in a kind of strained silence, watching Shorty Gibbs.

Yes sir, Shorty told himself, it sure was a wonder how important an out-of-work mail rider could get in such a short time.

A huge shadow fell in front of him as he was about to step into the street. The kind of shadow that only Tooms could throw.

Shorty gazed thoughtfully at the faces of Milo and the three ranchers. "Marshal," he said, "did you ever see four guiltier-lookin' gents than the ones standin' there in front of the cafe?"

"I never seen four more dangerous ones," Tooms rumbled. "You ever see that quiet look a cottonmouth gives you just before he strikes? That's the look they're givin' you now."

"I know," Shorty said with an indifference that he didn't feel. "Yesterday they just wanted me out of the

Panhandle, and was even willin' to pay me for goin'. Now I'm takin' the notion that they've got somethin' more serious in mind."

Tooms grunted, hesitated, then said, "A tinker just drove in from Tascosa. Took the short cut down south and made the ford at Gyp Creek. Recollect that mutton punchin' pal of yours?"

Shorty glanced up sharply. "What about him?"

"Dead," Tooms said bluntly but not cruelly—in the way of a man who hated to draw out as mean and sorry a thing as murder.

Shorty stared at him, swallowing with some difficulty. "Go on."

"The tinker smelled it first," Tooms said with velvet softness. "The sheep. They'd been shot, most of them, then soaked in coal oil and set afire. The wagon was given the same treatment, and so was the mule . . ."

"And the old man?" It might have been someone else asking—Shorty didn't recognize the voice as his own.

Tooms heaved a sigh. "The old man too."

For one long, silent moment Shorty fixed his arrow gaze on the four faces on the other side of the street. "Who else but the cowmen would want to kill a harmless old man like that!" Well, an inner voice reminded him, not completely harmless, maybe. Remembering that young cowhand spread-eagled in the creek bottom. Obviously the line rider had had some second thoughts about the incident. And he hadn't wasted any time getting the story to his boss.

Shorty closed his eyes for just a moment, tightly, too sick with the fact of being Shorty Gibbs for talking. The old man had saved his life. And how had Shorty repaid him?—by bullheadedly managing things so that Bohannan was almost sure to run head-on into the power and the wrath of the cowmen. *Bohannan would be alive right now if I hadn't turned that kid puncher loose!*

Tooms looked as if he had been reading his thoughts. "You know somethin' about this, Gibbs?"

"There's your killers across the street!" he said hoarsely. "And this time I can prove it." In blunt, hammerlike words, he had described the scene as he had found it in the creek bottom.

Tooms listened silently, gazing with apparent indifference at the cowmen. "Don't you see it, Tooms? This time I can *prove* who the killers are. That young line rider of English's—when I get my hands on him he'll be glad enough to tell you about it!"

"I got a notion," the big marshal purred, "that gettin' your hands on that rider won't be no simple matter. If what you say is true, I figure that puncher is right now on a fast horse headin' for the Indian Nations to get hisself lost. Or, like your mutton punchin' pal, he might be coyote bait hisself. Men that get to be big-brand cowmen don't have any special squeamishness about killin'."

There was a dangerous glint in Shorty's eyes. "You ain't goin' to do a thing about it? You're goin' to let them get away with it?"

"Right now," the marshal said wearily, "I aim to ride out to Gyp Creek to see if the tinker's story had any frills on it. I think maybe you'd better come with me."

Shorty got the pinto saddled and met Tooms at the wagon yard end of the street, not because Tooms had slyly ordered it, but because he realized that the marshal was probably right about the line rider, Bert Stoufer. When Stoufer realized what a stir he had caused he would be only too willing to make himself scarce. Either that, or, as Tooms had suggested, the youth himself was now so much coyote bait, like Bohannan. Either way, there went Shorty's "proof."

2

Even before they sighted the green cottonwoods that defined the creek the sickening odor of burned flesh and wool rose up to meet them.

The scene was like a battlefield on which there had been a bloody and one-sided engagement. A shroud of smoke lay in soft, oily layers on the valley. The skeleton of the wagon still smoldered, and the only things left whole were a few pieces of metal hardware such as bow brackets and steel tires from the wheels.

The carcasses of sheep, blackened and still smoldering also, dotted the grassy slope. And a few animals, dead but unburned, lay like huge cotton puffs in a deep green patch of mullein. Beyond the dead sheep, where the clayey bank fell suddenly away to the water, they saw Mary Ann, or what was left of her, blackened and bloated and as rigid as iron.

"Well," Shorty said at last, as though the single word had been wrenched from his throat. They nudged their animals and rode into the softly rolling layers of smoke.

They found the old man's body, unburned, in the weed patch between the white sheep bodies and the wagon. "Looks like they burned everything between the wagon and the mullein patch," Tooms purred with velvety softness. "Must of run out of coal oil when they come to the weeds."

Shorty said nothing. There were no words to describe the fire of his own, the one in his brain.

Before leaving Hardrow the marshal had thoughtfully lashed to his saddle a castoff Army trenching tool. Now he got down and silently began to work on a grave.

"That old man saved my hide," Shorty said at last in a tone that caused Tooms to pause in his digging. "I'd of made coyote bait myself, if it hadn't of been for him."

"Get down," Tooms said sharply, "and give a hand."

"We can't bury him here, like this."

"You know a better place? Wouldn't be much sense haulin' him into town, would it? Most likely he never cared much for towns anyhow."

Shorty gave every word solemn and individual attention. At last he got down, took the small shovel from the marshal's hands and began to dig. Tooms

took the nervous horses downstream and tied them—
so much death all around was making them spooky.

With professional thoroughness the marshal
searched the ground that the raiders had littered with
so much killing. He was not a squeamish man, and
this was not the first time he had seen wanton
slaughter and burning, nor was it the first time he had
seen a dead mutton puncher in cow country—never-
theless, he was shocked. For four years he had rested
comfortably in the belief that cowmen and sheepmen
had learned something from the last bloodletting. He
had been wrong.

This, he told himself more than once, ain't none of
my business, when you get right down to it. It's the
county sheriff's business.

But the county sheriff was where the votes were.
Tooms knew too well what would happen if he made
a complaint in the usual way. The request for aid
would somehow get lost or mislaid. The sheriff
wouldn't have the men to spare, until maybe election
time rolled around again, and then it wouldn't make
any difference.

Tooms put the county officials out of his mind. He
covered the ground step by step, recovering cartridge
cases and bits of glass vinegar jugs and a canvas
waterbag that had lately contained coal oil. He studied
hoofprints, and followed a set of tracks upstream but
lost it in all the trampling of Bohannan's woollies.
When he returned to the mullein patch a grim and
sweating Shorty Gibbs was smoothing the sides of a

nearly completed grave. He wiped his face on his sleeve and climbed out. "You find anything?"

"Two sets of tracks, but I lost them." If they looked long enough they could probably pick the tracks up again, but Tooms knew that it wouldn't be worth the time. The two riders would have made for the creek, split up and drowned their trail in gyp water. "Some .45 shell cases, and some from a rifle. But that don't mean anything since everybody's took to wearin' guns again."

Shorty hunkered beside the new grave, sunk deep in his own thoughts. "How long you figure it's been?" he said at last. "Maybe four, five hours, the way I see it. The tinker must of come by just about the time the job was finished. Maybe even before it was finished—that could account for the reason Bohannan and some of the sheep wasn't burned."

Tooms grunted.

"That," Shorty's thought continued, "would be just about time for that kid line rider to get to Spur head-quarters, spread the word about his treatment by the old man, and . . ."

"That's all guess work," Tooms said wearily.

"For you, maybe." Shorty looked up at the towering lawman.

"You're on dangerous ground, Gibbs," the marshal said flatly, "if you're thinkin' of layin' this at the feet of John English."

Surprisingly, Shorty only looked at him.

Silently, they buried the old man and filled the grave, and at no time did Shorty speak. They stood for a moment, gazing at the rounded mound of raw earth.

"I ain't much of a hand," Tooms said at last, "but seems like one of us ought to say something over him."

"It ain't talk he wants," Shorty said. "Words ain't goin' to satisfy that old man."

"Look here, Gibbs." There was a note of worry in the marshal's voice. "What're you nursin' in that schemin' head of yours?"

Shorty bared his teeth in what might have been a grin but wasn't. "Just thinkin'."

It was a hot, unpleasant ride back to Hardrow, and by the time they got there darkness had once again settled on the town. There was very little activity in the street, but several cow horses were tied up in front of Phil Sublet's Great Western Saloon.

Tooms grunted. "You don't reckon Phil's stopped waterin' his whiskey, do you?"

"More likely the cowmen don't care for the company Goldie Vale's keepin' nowadays, so Sublet's catchin' some of the Plug Hat trade." Shorty kneed in at the rack in front of Goldie's place.

Tooms said, "You don't aim to act the fool, any more'n usual, I hope."

Shorty grinned unpleasantly and said nothing. He stepped into the saloon where Goldie Vale slumped in boredom at the end of the bar. At first he thought the place was completely empty, but as he came into the lamplit interior he saw the Association man, Sam Milo, at one of the back tables.

"Just as well you ain't got a job," Goldie told him. "You wouldn't have time to work at it, what with all the prowlin' you do." She gazed steadily at his face, seeing things that Tooms had half-noticed—the taut, fiddlestring lines around the mouth, the bluish pouching beneath the eyes. "You found the old man, I guess."

Shorty nodded.

Goldie opened a bottle and poured in two glasses. "On the house," she said.

Shorty downed it and gave it a few seconds to warm his insides. "What's the Association man doin' here? All the cowmen are up at the Great Western."

"Maybe he likes to drink by hisself." She grinned acidly. "And this is a good place for it."

"How long's he been here?"

"Maybe two hours—ever since him and John English and a few Spur hands rode into town around sundown."

Shorty took a deep, thoughtful breath and did not object when Goldie poured another round. "You still got the Widow Courtney boardin' with you?"

"The widow," she said with just the slightest touch of acid, "has been tryin' to get back to Tascosa ever since you and Tooms rode out this mornin'. But her horse is over at the wagon yard down with the colic, according to the hostler. And her buckboard, so Murph Hogan told her, has got a busted axle, and he ain't right sure that he's got everything it takes to fix it."

Shorty stared. "Seems like some folks find Hardrow a mighty hard place to get out of. For others it's just as hard to stay." He glanced back at Sam Milo, but his thoughts were still with Mrs. Courtney. "I've been givin' the widow considerable thought, but I ain't much of a hand at judgin' women. How does she strike you?"

Goldie hesitated, gazing into her glass. "She's a queer one. Last night she was helpless and hurt like she had just had a mountain fall on her. This mornin' she—well, she did seem a lot less miserable for a spell. Then, after you and Tooms rode off and she learned about her horse and hack, she's been plain scared."

Shorty thought about this for several seconds, then silently downed the second shot of whiskey and walked back to where the Association man was seated.

"Looks a little funny, don't it, Milo? You doin' your drinkin' here while your pals take their business to the Great Western." He looked sharply at Milo's drawn face and saw that the Widow Courtney wasn't the only scared person in Hardrow.

"Sit down, Gibbs. I've been waitin' for you."

Shorty dropped into a chair. "That makes it handy,

because I've been wantin' to ask you about that side-kick of yours that got his neck stretched the other night. You did know that Courtney worked for the Association, didn't you?"

Milo wiped his thin mouth with the back of his hand. "I didn't know Courtney. I never heard of him till he got hisself in trouble here."

"Funny," Shorty drawled. "His widow claims he was a detective doin' undercover work for the head office."

Milo was sweating freely. He got out a handkerchief and mopped his face. "I don't believe a thing that woman says. And I don't think Courtney—if that was his name—worked for the Association. We'll soon know . . . I've sent off a letter to the head office . . ."

"So has Hoyt Tooms," Shorty said, taking a certain dry pleasure in seeing the Association man squirm. "And the postmaster in Tascosa. And maybe the county sheriff and other officials."

Milo's forehead glistened and he mopped it again. It was a warm night—but it wasn't that warm. Shorty said abruptly, "What did you want to see me about?"

The detective pocketed the handkerchief and became grimly businesslike. "You're playin' a losin' game, Gibbs. Nobody plagues cowmen like John English and lives to brag about it."

"Did English send you to tell me that?"

"He don't know anything about it." Milo drew a deep breath. "What is it you want, Gibbs? It don't make sense that anybody'd go stirring up trouble just for the hell of it."

"Is that what I'm doin', Milo, stirrin' up trouble?"

Milo ignored the sarcasm. "English offered you money, and you wouldn't have it. If it ain't money, what is it? Position? A job, maybe, that would set you up with best kind of folks—somewheres else than the Panhandle, of course."

"Of course," Shorty said dryly. Milo was beginning to interest him. "You and your pals are hard folks to understand, Milo. You just won't believe that some-times a man'll fight for somethin' that he can't bank."

Milo stared hard, his teeth bared. "You know what I'm talkin' about."

"Maybe," Shorty said cautiously, "but I'd rather hear it said."

The Association man hesitated, still sweating. "We don't know why, but we know that you and the old mutton puncher was in cahoots against the cowmen. Maybe because he brought you in off the prairie when you got yourself shot—the whys of the matter ain't important. But now the old man's dead. . . ."

"How'd you know that?" Shorty asked sharply.

"Everybody knows it. The tinker's spread the story over half the county by this time."

The belief that fear, when it was strong enough, was a thing that could actually be smelled, was no mere superstition. Shorty could smell it now; it radiated from Milo like waves of heat from desert rocks. The Association man swallowed hard and rushed into the spiel that he had prepared for the occasion. "Listen to me, Gibbs, because this'll be the last proposition you'll get. Some folks hereabouts ain't as patient as I am—they ain't so squeamish about how they stop a man that gets in their way—just so they stop him."

Shorty was listening, fascinated. "All right," Milo continued. "I know a fellow over at Fort Worth that can set you up in a good job at the head office. You won't be a nobody, the way you are here. You'll amount to somethin'. Money in your pocket, Gibbs, high-steppin' horses, fancy rigs, pretty women. All yours if you act reasonable."

"How reasonable, exactly?"

"Just keep your mouth shut and get out of Hardrow. Right now."

"Tonight?"

"Yes."

"What," Shorty asked, "is the big hurry?"

"You know that as well as I do, Gibbs."

Shorty stared grimly into space while Milo fidgeted. Milo and his friends were giving him credit for brains and information that he didn't own. It was a queer feeling, having someone afraid of you and not knowing why. Shorty decided to look for the clue in another direction.

"It ain't goin' to solve your problem, even if I pull out like you want. There's still Tooms. He knows about as much as I do."

"I know," Milo said impatiently. "But lawmen don't get much in the way of money. With you out of the way, he'll listen to reason."

Shorty looked thoughtful. "I see." But he didn't see at all.

"What," he asked bluntly, "if Tooms decides not to listen to reason."

Milo sighed. "If it comes to that—well, town marshals get killed every day."

Shorty could not control the dangerous glint in his eyes, but Milo appeared not to notice. "What's it goin' to be, Gibbs?" He had mistaken the glint of anger for the glassy look of greed.

"I'll . . . need time to think it over."

"There ain't any time left. You pull out tonight or not at all." He grinned. He was sure of himself now, as Shorty half opened his mouth but did not speak. He had Shorty Gibbs on the run.

The Association man squinted quizzically but was still grinning when Shorty kicked his chair back and stood up. "Mister," Shorty said coldly, "you come at a bad time. I've just been out plantin' a friend of mine. It's been a hard day, my fur's been rubbed the wrong way, and I'm a little short on patience. And, if you want the honest truth of the matter, I just don't like the look of your face."

Then, with taut, bunched muscles suddenly released, he hit Sam Milo in the middle of his spreading grin.

The Association man looked stunned and hurt, but most of all, outraged—definitely outraged—as his head snapped back and he lost his balance. The chair turned over with him, dumping him heavily on the saloon floor. He scrambled to his hands and knees, staring wildly about. Gingerly, he touched his bloody mouth, then, in panic, began crawdadding away from Shorty.

"Get up," Shorty snarled. "I ain't half through with you yet!"

Still on hands and knees, Milo was scrambling for the front of the saloon, knocking tables awry and upsetting chairs in his hasty retreat.

From her place behind the bar Goldie watched the eruption with an air of resignation. "Listen, Gibbs!" the Association man pleaded. "Listen to me!" But Shorty stalked him mercilessly, like a homesteader stalking a gopher with a grubbing hoe. He grabbed Milo by the collar of his shirt and hauled him roughly to his feet.

Milo stood almost a head over him, but Shorty Gibbs, in his anger, did not have the look of a small man. "You listen to me, Association man," he hissed, punching Milo in the gut by way of punctuation. Milo half doubled and reeled back against the bar. In desperation he grabbed awkwardly for his .45. Unceremoniously, Shorty knocked it out of his hand. In cold fury, he struck Milo again, this time alongside his left ear, and Milo grabbed at the bar for support, but only fleetingly. Suddenly he pushed himself away, kicked a chair between Shorty and himself and ran for the door.

Goldie Vale spread her arms elaborately. "Well, there goes the only payin' customer I've had all day."

Shorty stood staring at the rattling batwings and, beyond, the darkness that had swallowed the Association detective.

"I don't guess," Goldie said wryly, "it would do any good to ask what that was all about."

Shorty pulled his hat down on his forehead and followed Sam Milo out of the saloon. "No," he heard Goldie saying to herself, "I guess it wouldn't."

4

Marshal Hoyt Tooms was in his one-cell calaboose methodically going through several months of accumulated correspondence. By the leaping light of a tallow candle he scrutinized a goodly number of "wanted" bills as well as the communications of other lawmen.

In the outside darkness someone turned away from the street and headed toward the calaboose. From the quick, agitated sound of bootheels on hard clay, Tooms didn't have to guess who the visitor was. When Shorty Gibbs was angry even the sound of his footsteps proclaimed the fact.

Tooms raised his big head and asked wearily, "What is it now, Gibbs?"

"I just had a little set-to with Sam Milo." The candle on the floor cast unexpected and vaguely disturbing shadows against the rock walls. Shorty stepped inside, fixing a slitted gaze on the pile of papers that Tooms had been poring over.

"Just wanted to make sure," the marshal offered, "that I hadn't overlooked some piece of skullduggery in these parts—anything that might explain why the Association would send an unknown detective to work in Hardrow. I didn't find anything." He blocked the "wanted" bills as if they were oversized playing cards and put them on the floor. "What's this about you and Milo?"

"Did you know," Shorty answered with usual obliqueness, "that you could be a rich man?"

The marshal smiled tautly, as though he had just bitten into an unripe persimmon. "Interestin' if true."

"All you have to do is work up a good case of bad memory. Forget about the things that's been happenin' around here lately. Like the thing we saw out on Gyp Creek today. Forget you ever seen it. Forget about the missing mail pouches, and those reports that Courtney was supposed to of made out. After all, we don't actually *know* they was reports, do we? We only got the widow's word for that, and *she* don't seem too concerned about it."

"Whose proposition is this?" Tooms asked blandly.

"Milo's, but he's talkin' for the cowmen."

Tooms grunted. "What else am I supposed to do to get myself rich?"

"You might be called on to explain a lynchin' to some county officials and maybe the Association. That shouldn't be too hard, seein' that the widow seems ready to go along with it."

With quiet patience, Tooms waited.

Shorty prompted him. "Well?"

"Would I be the only rich man in town," he asked dryly, "or would the two of us divide that honor?"

Shorty's mouth stretched in what might have been a grin. "You'd have that honor all to yourself. If I make the deal, it's on the condition that I pull stakes."

"Do you aim to take it?"

"I ain't decided yet."

"I think you have," Tooms said in his big cat voice. "And I think you're tryin' to haze me into English's corral just to make yourself feel good for not takin' blood money."

Tooms came to his feet, expecting at least a loud expression of indignation, but Shorty only grunted. He had turned and was gazing toward the street. Two horsebackers rode out of the darkness into the weak, suffused light of the street. "Vance and Corry?"

The marshal moved to the doorway. "Can't tell in this light." He returned to the cell, gathered up his papers and blew out the candle. "If you think of any more schemes to get us rich," he said dryly, "be sure to let me know." He walked away from the jail, moving down the broad alley behind the business houses.

For some time Shorty remained in thoughtful silence. He felt a little better about Tooms, but now another worry had come to plague him. When a cowman wanted something, usually he asked once, then reached for his gun. The thing I don't understand, Shorty argued to himself, is why English don't just finish me off with a bullet.

That's what you'd expect a big brand rancher to do if he wanted to shut somebody up. It wasn't like them to sit and pass a hand, and to keep on passin', while they were holding all the cards. Shorty wasn't fooling himself. It would be no big trick to kill him, if English wanted him dead. For that matter, the same thing could be said about Tooms.

As for Milo—he might be somebody to the Association office boys back at Fort Worth, but here in the Panhandle he was just somebody to run errands for John English. This was a cow family play, not Milo's.

Shorty walked slowly toward the rosy glow that marked the Plug Hat. The saloon was still deserted. The cow convention was at the far end of the street, at the Great Western.

He headed toward the Great Western, like iron dust drawn to a magnet. He could hear the noise now, the loud talk and the laughter. Maybe they were laughing about Seth Bohannan.

The last two horsebackers to enter town had tied up at the end of the rack, a short distance from the saloon. Shorty recognized the animals as the ones that Vance and Nate Corry had been riding. He studied the horses for a moment, then stepped down from the plankwalk and inspected them closer. The two saddle guns were still in their boots. Shorty remembered that he still carried Nate's revolver in his waistband, and Vance's pearl-handled Peacemaker was in the pinto's saddle pocket.

As he moved in closer to the animals he became aware of something that chilled him. It was nothing seen, nothing heard, but a certain odor that clung like death to the deep wool of the Indian saddle blankets and even to the hide of the unbrushed horses. It was faint and not easy to detect because the same stench of charred wool and flesh probably clung to himself. But it was there all the same, and unmistakable.

Deliberately, Shorty slammed a door on anger. He considered the discovery coldly. It was possible that Vance and the foreman had ridden down to Bohannan's burned-out camp just for entertainment, well after the killing. On the other hand it was just as possible that they had been there at the beginning. . . .

He stood there for some time, his nostrils flaring. The sickish faintly sweet stench seemed to soak into his pores. There was another scent that he couldn't quite place, a foreign scent, different altogether from the mingled odors of death.

Then a voice from nowhere, as it seemed, called softly, sneeringly, "If you got it in mind to steal them horses, little man, forget it. Vance English would squash you like you was a heelfly grub."

Shorty wheeled in instant anger, searching the night for the voice. "Who said that!"

"Over here, little man . . ."

Now Shorty saw the blurred figure slouching in the dark alleyway between the Great Western and a feed store. "Come out where I can see you, if you ain't afraid."

The man laughed unpleasantly. "Oh, I ain't afraid, little man. But I'm used to doin' whatever I feel like, not what some sawed-off saddle tramp tells me to do."

Shorty started toward the voice, the muscles of his shoulders bunched and cramping. "Friend," he said softly, "if you're lookin' for trouble . . ."

"Well, now!" The laugh again. "And what if I was? I'd have to look mighty hard, wouldn't I, because there ain't hardly enough of you for a real man to fool with."

Every time he heard those words a new ripple of anger went over him. But he stepped up to the plankwalk and made himself pause and tried to shrug it off—that much, at least, was to his credit. "Mister, why don't you just go off behind the saloon and sleep it off. I don't even know you—at least I don't think I do."

"What's the matter, little man? You short on guts, like everything else?"

That did it. Shorty clamped his jaws hard enough to crack bones and marched stiffly into the alley. Too late, he noted the size of the man—not that it would have made any difference. Almost as big as Tooms, the man towered over Shorty, his big fists hanging like loose-swinging clubs.

So Vance, Shorty thought, would crush him like a heelfly grub, would he? Then why wasn't he out here doing his own fighting instead of sending one of his riders.

"Well, now," the unpleasant voice rumbled, "the

runt of the litter's got some grit after all, has he?"
Shorty swung with all the anger-fired strength in his
whang-tough frame.

The big man grunted in surprise and pain. Shorty
felt the impact all the way to his shoulder. His fist for
a moment was pleasantly numb. The giant fell back a
few steps, pawing in glazed amazement at his bloody
mouth. Shorty hit him again, but the enemy was in
temporary retreat and the blow landed on the muscular
chest. He felt no softness there; the man was as solid
as an oak trunk, and Shorty knew that he would have
to finish it quick if he hoped to finish it at all.

By this time the enemy had stopped retreating and
was gathering himself for attack. Shorty swung again,
but this time his fist was knocked aside with appalling
ease. For a moment the man's face caught a bit of
vagrant light, and Shorty stared. It was not a pleasant
sight.

It was a battered, hard-used face, flat as a Kiowa's,
with a flattened potato of a nose and a bloody mouth
and a missing front tooth. The first shock of having to
defend himself against a man not much more than half
his size and weight had passed. Now the giant was
grinning, savoring a foretaste of what was to come.
Except for a bit of blood and a lost tooth, Shorty's
hardest punches seemed not to have bothered him at
all.

For the space of a second the piece of stray light
widened—maybe or just an instant—and in the act of
swinging again, Shorty froze.

He and the giant did not have the alley to themselves, as he had thought. Several men, maybe five or
six, stood back in the deep shadow against the feed
store, following the action mostly by sound. There
wasn't time for noting detail, but he did glimpse
Vance English's widely grinning face. And old John
English looking grim and determined and not amused
at all. And Sam Milo, with all his fears and frustra-
tions and misgivings crowded into one razor scratch
of a smile. Then the moment of light blinked out.
Somebody—maybe English himself—said, "Make it
a good job, Hud. A good one, you hear me?"

Shorty sensed the man's dull-like lunge before he
actually saw or heard it. He hopped to one side and
began to fall back. Not fast enough. A huge fist caught
him a glancing blow, like an iron maul caressing his
cheek. The force of it almost lifted him off the ground.
His head snapped back. He was deafened by a great
clamoring and ringing in his ears. The left side of his
face was suddenly numb and wooden.

Shorty had come up against big men before, but
none like this one. He hit like a Comanche with a war
ax. Shorty was spun half-around, stumbled, almost
went to the ground. Boys, he thought idiotically, this
ain't goin' to do. It ain't goin' to do at all!

But this man called Hud was appallingly fast on his
feet. He danced a wide circle around Shorty, cutting
him off from the street. The giant said happily, "Ain't
no use tryin' to run, little man. You might as well stand
and take your whippin'."

"That'll be a day to remember!" Shorty snarled. Hud was lunging again.

Shorty darted to his right, away from that huge right fist, and almost ran head-on into Hud's left. It whistled toward him like solid shot from a brass Napoleon. Shorty, to the giant's amazement, threw himself to the ground, but not in time to escape another glancing blow that paralyzed his left shoulder and sent him sprawling. Someone in the unseen audience was laughing. That would be Vance. Someone else was calling tensely but quietly, "Not all at once, Hud." And still another voice: "Stretch it out a little. Let him know we mean business."

There wasn't much doubt in Shorty's mind that they meant business. He was rattled and hurt. He couldn't believe that any man, no matter how big, could manhandle him the way Hud was manhandling him. But boys, he told himself as he lay helplessly on the ground, that's the sorry truth of the matter. He's whippin' hell out of me and there ain't a thing in the world I can do about it.

Well, the thought continued on a slightly different plain, nothin' *fair and square,* that is!

It seemed that he rolled and tumbled for a long time before finally rattling to a stop. His left arm hung at his side as unfeeling as a plow handle. Hud was standing over him, gazing down at him with that bloody grin. "Get up, little man, I ain't nigh through with you yet."

Vance laughed, but the rest of the watchers were

116

silent. Hud appeared faintly amused but not angry. Shorty realized that there was nothing personal in this on the giant's part; he was just a hired hand doing a job. He understood that Hud was merely a tool in the hands of the cowmen, to be used as they saw fit, like a gun, or a rope.

"If he don't get up, haul him up," John English said in a tone as flat as a side of beef.

Even then Shorty wondered why they didn't kill him and settle the matter once and for all, if they were so all-fired anxious to get rid of him. Why do it slow and hard when it could be done so quick and easy with a bullet?

Hud tongued the bloody gap where a front tooth had been and began to lose some of his good humor. "What's it goin' to be?" he asked with a certain bleakness. "You goin' to get up and take your whippin' like a man, or do I have to . . ."

Shorty, with an inward sigh of resignation, said, "Oh I'll get up, all right. Don't never have any doubts about *that*."

Vance chuckled softly as Shorty attempted to support himself on his numb left hand and fell over on his back. Angrily, he jackknifed forward and shoved himself to his knees. Still tonguing the bloody space between his teeth, Hud waited with knotted fists.

All right, boys, Shorty thought coldly, if this is the way you want it, this here's the way she's goin' to be. We're goin' to stop playin' this game like little gentlemen.

Bracing his right elbow on his right knee, he shoved himself to his feet. As he did, he grasped the butt of Nate Corry's .45 and jerked it out of his waistband.

Shorty pointed the muzzle at Hud's gut and grinned crookedly. The giant looked stunned. He stared at the revolver. "I ain't got a gun!" He inched back a little into the light, and spread his arms to show that he was unarmed.

An angry sound arose from the spectators. "Look here, Gibbs," John English snapped, "you shoot an unarmed man and you'll be stretchin' rope before mornin'. I give you my personal word on it."

"If I got to pick between hangin' and gettin' my brains beat out, I'd just as soon take hangin'."

"I can shoot you right where you stand," English said grimly. "The law would back me up, and you know it."

Well, Shorty told himself, it's time to play the ace. "If you had the gall to kill me, English, you would of done it a long time before now."

They stared at him with eyes like bullets, but nobody went for his gun. Slowly, and very carefully, Shorty maneuvered Hud so that his back was to the ranchers. Somebody—Vance, more than likely—suddenly decided to kick down Shorty's mysterious vale of protection that, for some reason, the cowmen were afraid to broach. With a start of alarm, Emery Straiter snapped, "Don't do it, boy!"

And John English snarled, "You fool! Don't you think you've caused enough trouble already!" Then, with a tone of resignation, English said, "Throw the gun down, Gibbs. You can walk away with your hide."

Shorty snorted. "Not likely." He punched Hud in his hard gut and moved him to one side. "Come out in the light where I can get a look at you, gents."

Nobody moved or made a sound. Again Shorty rammed the tough giant with the .45, failing to see the silent half snarl that curled Hud's puffy lip. Hud's fear of firearms was not without limit. To Shorty's amazement he saw his gunhand being knocked roughly to one side—and then he learned how it felt to be shot with a buffalo gun at close range.

Hud's big right fist couldn't have traveled more than six inches, then hooked viciously into his ribs. All the air rushed out of Shorty's lungs. He discovered himself flying back toward the saloon, desperately working his legs and flailing his arms in an attempt to keep his feet. He smashed into the saloon wall and the dry timber cracked with the sound of lightning striking an oak stump. He felt himself falling. He stared at his right hand, surprised to see he still had the revolver.

Hud, his wide face twisted, charged down on him like a maddened range bull. Shorty didn't dare move away from the wall for fear of collapsing. He worked his mouth and made strange desperate little sounds in the effort to breathe. He could almost feel his face turning blue. A core of white heat in his chest began to spread to his shoulders and arms. For all he knew, the shock of Hud's punch might have crippled his breathing permanently.

A voice hoarse with excitement—Milo's—called, "Finish him, Hud! Finish him!"

It couldn't have taken Hud longer than a second to cross the short space to where Shorty had crashed against the saloon wall, but to Shorty it passed with nightmarish slowness. He worked his mouth and continued to make those small howling sounds, but air would not enter his deflated lungs. All right, gents, he thought coldly, if this is the way she's goin' to be. . . .

He raised his gunhand, and in that small part of a second that was left to him, his mind worked with startling speed. He sensed the amazement that had suddenly struck the onlookers. They're waitin' for me to shoot him, he thought. They *want* me to shoot him. They figure that'll solve all their problems. And maybe it would. I don't even know what their problems are. But they figure they can get me hung nice and legal for killin' an unarmed man. . . .

It was time to act. From some black, angry room in his mind he found strength to lunge outside the bullet-like path of Hud's first rush. Fast as the big man was, for an instant Shorty was faster. With studied savagery he slashed down with the barrel of the .45. There was a faintly hollow and hugely satisfying thud, like a solid thump against an overripe melon, as the pistol barrel came down on the giant's head.

The big man fell without a sound, the great hulk collapsing on the spot like an empty suit of clothes.

Shorty grinned with a kind of wildness—a prairie

lobo run down and trapped in a box canyon—at the stunned group of cowmen. "All right, gents, which one of you aims to be next!" For the moment he failed to notice that he was breathing again, gulping great quantities of air into his aching lungs.

"Come on!" he snarled in quiet rage. Wild horses couldn't drag him out of the alley now.

It was the foreman, Nate Corry, who was the first to break the stunned silence. He stepped forward, out of deep darkness into lesser darkness, carrying his gunbelt and holstered revolver in his hand. Now I don't feel so bad about takin' his gun, Shorty thought grimly, seein' as how he's got plenty more where this one came from.

The foreman casually flung the belt and weapon away from him. "Here's another chance, Gibbs, to shoot an unarmed man."

Shorty's wolfish grin widened. "I don't figure I need a gun to handle the likes of you, Corry." Idiotically, copying the foreman's theatrics, he lobbed his own .45 into the dirt beside the saloon.

Corry laughed. "I always knowed you was a fool, Gibbs, but I never knowed until now that you was *all* fool."

Shorty blinked, not at first understanding how thoroughly he had let anger and pride destroy him. Then, as Corry came toward him, Shorty was aware of other movement in the alley. The cowmen were no longer clustered in one place. There was movement to his right, and to his left. He wheeled suddenly and saw

Vance and one of the Spur riders cutting him off from the street. Nate and Sam Milo were coming toward him from the other end of the alley. On his left was John English and Emery Straiter. On his right was Paul Maston and one of his riders.

"So this is the way she's goin' to be," Shorty heard himself saying, in awe of his own stupidity.

Sam Milo grinned. "This is the way she's goin' to be, Gibbs."

They closed in slowly, quietly, and with singleness of purpose that Shorty Gibbs fully understood. "Now look here, boys, this ain't hardly what I'd call a sportin' proposition!"

But John English had offered once to let him pull out with his whole hide—it didn't look like the offer was going to be repeated.

CHAPTER SEVEN

1

The last clear thought that Shorty remembered having was, I wonder where the hell Tooms goes to hide whenever somebody needs a marshal? Then Corry and Milo came at him from one direction and Vance and the Spur rider from the other, the Maston hand joining in from one side.

Corry was the first to swing. Shorty ducked taking the light punch on his shoulder and countered with a fist in the foreman's gut. Corry, like most men who fancied themselves gunmen, was vain of his hands. This was a point in Shorty's favor, but not enough to overcome the odds of four other men who were not hindered by such vanity.

The old ranchers, Shorty saw as he jumped back from a wild swing taken by Sam Milo, were declining an active part in the to-do. English, Straiter, and Maston stood as glowering guards on Shorty's flanks to prevent his escaping. Or, Shorty thought, in a brand-new rage, maybe they just don't want to get my blood on their ninety-dollar boots.

As he jumped back from Milo either Vance or the Spur hand hit him from behind. An ironlike fist that exploded stars behind his right ear. Then, with admirable efficiency, they bore down on him. He lashed out wildly, bruising and skinning and bloodying his fists, but the final outcome was never in the slightest doubt.

They downed him as methodically as an experienced crew might down a bawling calf at a branding fire. They hammered him down inch by inch, like a piling being driven into stubborn ground.

And when they had him on the ground they slammed the sharp toes of their boots into his already tender ribs. In a kind of numb disbelief, Shorty stared up at them. None of them, with the possible exception of Vance English, seemed to take any special pleasure in what he was doing. Like the giant Hud, they were just hired hands doing a job, and doing it very well too, Shorty thought blearily. Unconsciousness settled around his vagrant, half-formed thoughts, smothering them one by one.

2

He came awake a little at a time and gradually entered a sickish world entirely surrounded by blank, uncurious faces. Vance English, as usual, was the exception. He was grinning widely; his eyes glittered. Shorty noticed with little satisfaction that one of Vance's eyes was discolored and swollen almost shut.

John English, who was hunkered down on his heels studying Shorty's face by the light of a flaring match—studying it with the fixity of a big cat studying a kicking bug—said to the others, "He's comin' alive, I think."

The match went out and Shorty was blinded in the sudden darkness. "Here," Vance was saying with steely good humor, "this ought to do it." He held a beer schooner shoulder high and dribbled the lukewarm suds in Shorty's face.

Shorty spat and sputtered and tried to jerk himself erect. But he was pegged to the ground by a hundred needlesharp arrows of pain. When an old cowman makes up his mind to do somethin', he didn't go about it half way! He felt as if all his ribs were broken and the splintered ends punching through his side.

"You hear me, Gibbs?" English asked flatly.

Shorty stared at the old man with murder in his heart.

"I guess you do," the rancher said thoughtfully. "If you're hurtin', it's your own fault. You oughtn't to be so damn bullheaded. You ought to pay more attention to what folks tell you." He grasped Shorty's shoulder, and pain rattled against Shorty's sides like dice in a cup. "You hear me, Gibbs?"

"I heard you the first time," Shorty grated.

"Don't feel so good, I guess."

Shorty started to snarl and the pain took his breath away.

"Yes," John English said thoughtfully, as if to himself. "This ain't my style, Gibbs, and I don't like it much, either. If it was up to me, why I'd just shoot you, and that would be the end of it."

"Who's it up to, if it ain't up to you?"

English gave him that catlike look and said, "It don't matter. You're leavin' Hardrow soon's you can ride."

"You right sure of that?" Shorty asked through clinched teeth.

"It's up to you. If you want another dose of what you got tonight, why just let me find you in Hardrow after tomorrow." He got to his feet, grunting. "How's Hud doin'?" he asked the gathering at large.

"Beginnin' to come around," somebody said.

"Let him draw his time when we get back to headquarters. I don't want a hand on my payroll that can't do what he's told. Tomorrow," he said, looking again at Shorty. With an abrupt nod he indicated that the business of the moment was finished.

"Old man!"

The rancher half-turned.

"I can't help wonderin'," Shorty said. "Why don't you just have me shot, the way you'd like to do? What is it about me that you're so scared of?"

"There ain't nothin' about you I'm scared of, Gibbs. Shootin' you wouldn't mean any more to me than shootin' a coyote."

"Then how come I'm still alive?"

Did the old man sag a little, or was it Shorty's imagination? Did the bunch of them stand a little less erect in their arrogance as they turned and headed for their horses?

Shorty had another try at getting up and decided it wasn't worth the price he'd have to pay in pain. Lay still, he told himself. Breathe light. Try not to do any more damage to your innards than you can help. Sooner or later somebody'll come this way and give you a hand . . . Maybe.

Part of the English train got their horses at the street rack, others went to the back alley behind the saloon where they had their animals staked. They left town in twos and threes, talking among themselves, conversationally—just a few ranchers and carefree cowhands in town for a little fun to break the monotony of range life.

The saloon was silent now—so silent that Shorty could hear the nervous pacing of Phil Sublet through the thin walls. Shorty called in a voice not much louder than a whisper, "Phil! Out here in the alley!"

He figured the chance of Phil's hearing him was small, and the chance that he would do anything, even if he did hear, was even smaller. Surprisingly, the barkeep appeared at the back door almost immediately.

"Gibbs? Whereabouts are you?"

"Over here, by the feed store."

Sublet stepped outside with a coal-oil lantern. He rounded the corner and stopped suddenly when he got his first look at Shorty. "What's the matter!" Shorty said in a whispered snarl. "Ain't you never seen blood before?"

Phil wiped his glistening forehead on his sleeve. "It's just that I never expected to find . . ." He started to say that he hadn't expected to find Shorty alive, but a small voice must have warned him.

"I guess," Shorty rasped, "you never heard the commotion out here."

"Never heard a blessed thing, Shorty," Sublet vowed, sounding as if he had both hands on his mother's Bible.

Shorty shut his eyes and ground his teeth. This was no time to blow up. He said in a faintly strangled tone, "See if you can find Tooms. Tell him I'd kind of like to see him, if it ain't too much trouble, and if he can spare the time."

Sublet shifted feet several times, sweating freely and wishing now that he had never left the saloon.

3

Shorty tried some experimental moving around while Sublet was looking for the marshal. His legs and arms were all right except for deep bruises. His breathing seemed to be a little freer now and the pain not quite so sharp.

By the light of Sublet's lantern he scanned the ground for the .45 that he had dropped. It wasn't there. Probably it was back in Nate Corry's holster. He tried once more to sit up, and once more the knives in his side told him it wasn't the thing to do.

He lay still, breathing lightly. There was a certain half-remembered stench in the air, a sweetish, oily odor, edged subtly with the smell of death. He raised his head, sniffing in the direction of the lantern—then he knew what it was. Coal oil.

Coal oil had been used in the burning of Bohannan's wagon and animals—that was the smell that had reminded him of death. But that wasn't all. Something else having to do with this particular scent lay just beyond the reach of his memory.

He squinted with the effort of remembering. Coal oil. Sheep. Death. Bohannan . . . Saddle.

Shorty's eyes opened wide. That was it; there had been the smell of coal oil on the rigs and horses belonging to Vance English and Nate Corry, along with the sooty smell of burned wool and flesh.

Tooms rounded the feed store corner and stopped abruptly when he saw Shorty's face in the lantern light.

"Goddam you, Tooms, where've you been hidin' this time, when there's trouble to be dealt with!"

Tooms grinned thinly. "So your mouth got you in hot water again, has it?"

"Anytime," Shorty said bitterly, "you get tired grinnin' like a peyote-eatin' Cheyenne squaw you can help me up from here—if it ain't goin' to put you out none."

"It won't put me out," the big marshal said blandly, "I was headin' this way anyhow when Phil Sublet found me. What happened?"

"Phil didn't tell you?"

"Said he didn't know."

Between spells of swearing Shorty related the story of the alley fight, more or less as it had happened.

"Hud," Tooms said thoughtfully, when Shorty first mentioned the flat-nosed giant by name. "That would be Hud Starr—claims he used to be a prize bare-knuckle fighter down in New Orleans. I didn't know he was workin' for Spur."

"He ain't any more," Shorty said with some small measure of satisfaction. "English fired him." He raised himself to his elbows and winced. "What I don't understand is why English would hire a bare-knuckle box fighter when gunhands come just as cheap and do their jobs a sight more permanent."

Tooms rubbed his great square chin and grunted. "Think you can walk?"

"The trick ain't in walkin'. The trick's in gettin' up off my back."

Tooms got his hands under Shorty's arms and lifted him as easily as he would lift a baby. Shorty gasped and swore as sweat in great beads broke out on his forehead. He rested against the saloon wall, getting his breath.

"How do you feel?" Tooms asked.

"Fine," Shorty grated. "Like all my ribs are busted and stickin' in my gizzard!"

Goldie Vale stared as the big marshal steered a shaken, white-faced Shorty Gibbs into the Plug Hat Saloon. "Mr. Gibbs," Tooms told her, "has had kind of a hard night."

Shorty held his anger because he didn't have the strength to turn it loose. Tooms guided him to a chair and eased him down to it. "I'll get some soap and water," Goldie said, staring at the numerous cuts and bruises on Shorty's face.

"Later," Tooms told her. "First thing we need is somethin' to bind him up with."

She hurried up the stairs to her quarters. In a few minutes she hurried down again, carrying a folded bedsheet. She was trailed by the nervous and pinch-faced widow of the late Ralph Courtney. While Tooms calmly stripped Shorty to the waist, Goldie and Mrs. Courtney ripped the lavender-scented sheet into uniform winding strips.

"Suck in your gut," Tooms said, "and let the air out of your lungs."

Shorty obeyed, gazing in amazement at all the activity he had caused. He even forgot to be embarrassed when Mrs. Courtney produced a bottle of witch hazel and applied the clear liquid to his bruised torso. Tooms took the white strips from Goldie and attended to the binding himself.

"How's that feel?" he asked when he had Shorty securely trussed.

"I can't breathe."

"Good." Tooms nodded with grim satisfaction. "The less you breathe the less trouble you'll get into."

"What happened?" Goldie asked worriedly as Tooms got Shorty back in his shirt. "You look like you been fightin' grizzlies with rocks and sticks."

Shorty glared but said nothing. Tooms folded his arms and stood looking down at him. "I got the notion," he said dryly, "that Mr. Gibbs has lost patience with the law hereabouts. What was your scheme, Gibbs? Just tramp into the saloon and start flailing at Vance English? Is that the way you figured to get the answer to things?"

Tooms took a deep breath and briefly repeated Shorty's version of the fight to Goldie. The drawn-faced Widow Courtney peered up at them with something more than normal interest. Her pale face was now stark white, and her gaze turned inward as she nervously twisted the remains of Goldie's bedsheet. After a while she realized that there was silence in the saloon and that the others were looking at her with puzzled eyes.

"When," she asked suddenly, her attention flitting past Shorty and on to Tooms, "do you think I can leave . . . ?"

"That depends on your animal and rig, ma'am. The blacksmith says the buckboard will take time to fix, but the horse ought to throw off the colic in a day or so."

Her eyes grew wide. "A day or so!" She looked as if she had just heard the pronouncement of her own death sentence.

4

It was later, much later, that Shorty lay in the dark and silent saloon, with a folded Indian blanket between him and the slate slab of the pool table.

Maybe, he thought grimly, the old mutton puncher had the right idea after all. Men like English and Maston and Straiter understood just one kind of language. Loaded guns and naked knives.

Every few minutes a reoccurring thought would drift across his mind. Why couldn't he drop it? Just pull out and leave Hardrow behind and be glad he was rid of it. With or without satisfaction for Seth Bohannan. The old man was dead and a long time buried and nothing could be done for him now . . .

Still, the old sheepman had very likely saved Shorty's life. That was a bald fact. Good or bad, smart or stupid, the fact remained that Shorty Gibbs had got himself into the debt of a dead man, and Shorty Gibbs was a man who paid his debts.

A shadow flitted on Plug Hat's plate-glass window. An unmistakable chill crept up Shorty's spine. He raised himself slightly, staring out at the darkened street. A summer moon cast a blue milk light on the buildings, light as thin as an old man's blood. Could that shadow have been his imagination? His head said yes. The cramp in his guts said no.

He felt along the side of the pool table until his hand touched the cold smoothness of Vance English's pearl-handled .45, and suddenly he was glad that he had made Tooms get it for him out of the saddle pocket.

Then he thought, "Wait a minute. The inside of this saloon must be as dark as a bear cave, lookin' in from the street." If anybody *was* looking in. If he wasn't just having a case of nerves. Up front a bit of moonlight sifted wanly through the glass, but even that light faded out far short of the pool table which was near the rear of the building.

So gentle down, he told himself. This ain't no time to get spooky.

But his common sense said one thing while he was doing something else. Dark or not, he suddenly didn't like the notion of being there on top of the pool table with nothing but clear glass between him and the street. With a sudden lurch that took his breath away, he threw himself forward. He swung his feet over the side of the table, felt for his boots and eased into them.

All right, he thought, panting rapidly, his heart thumping a sudden demand for oxygen that his constricted lungs could not deliver. So far, so good.

He eased himself from the table and quickly bunched the blanket into a lumpy tube—not much like the figure of a man, even if anybody could see it, but it would have to do.

Now that he was off the table, he doubted that he could get himself back on it, if it happened that he should stop jumping at shadows long enough to think about sleep. He began to feel foolish. What was he going to say in the morning when Goldie came down . . .

Something else flitted along the lower edge of the window. There was no mistake about it this time. And it was no shadow. Instinctively, Shorty dropped to the floor behind the end of the bar. The shock seemed to skyrocket a bright ball of pain through the top of his skull. He dropped the revolver, grabbed the footrail and ground his teeth until some of the pain subsided. Then he fumbled behind the footrail until he found the .45.

He waited.

And he waited some more. Seconds passed with incredible slowness. Minutes stretched into small eternities. He waited. Outside in the whey colored street everything was perfectly still. Still as the grave, quiet as death. Nothing moved. Nothing that he could see.

He waited. He began to get bored with waiting. Bored, and short of breath, and weary of the knives gouging at his innards. He began to relax. The notion that he was making a fool of himself began to haunt him. Then, quite suddenly, and even as he stared at it, the glass window exploded.

Three things happened so fast and close together that they seemed almost to happen at once. But the thing Shorty first noted was the exploding window.

The heavy glass shattered with the suddenness of a thunderclap. Glass, like sharp-edged ice, pelted the interior of the saloon. Then the street was thrown in sudden light, and Shorty thought for one stunned moment that the building had been hit by lightning. Lightning from a cloudless sky?

It was not lightning. The street continued to dance in a hot, reddish fire, and that was not the way of lightning. A realization of what must be happening seized Shorty by the throat. He grasped the top of the bar and pulled himself up against the points of knives.

A sputtering fireball looped in through the shattered window even before the splinters of glass had stopped falling. It landed in the center of the floor, garishly lighting the saloon's interior. Then, before Shorty could haul himself to the top of the bar and aim the revolver, a rifle from the street began to roar.

Shorty sensed more than saw the heavy slugs ripping through the roughly shaped blanket. Then it was over. Even before he could brace himself, cock the revolver and fire, it was over.

Suddenly there was nothing to shoot at. Nothing to see except the sullen fire on the floor and the blinding aftersight of muzzle flashes. He was on the verge of firing blindly when he sensed that it might be smart to let the would-be assassin think that the blanket had been the real thing.

At the top of the stairs the door to Goldie's quarters burst open. "It's all right," Shorty heard himself saying stupidly, between panting gulps for air, "It's just a torch. I'll put it out."

Goldie stared at him, a certain silent shrillness in her eyes. "Shorty," she wailed, "the place is on fire!"

"It's just a torch," he said again, this time with a touch of impatience. He pushed himself away from the bar and walked painfully toward the coal-oil soaked rag burning at the end of a stick. Then Mrs. Courtney appeared on the landing behind Goldie and screamed.

With eerie suddenness and silence, a sheet of fire rose up to cover the gaping window. Blue-red tongues licked through the cracks in the walls. Bright fingers of fire seized the painted walls and began to climb.

Shorty stared numbly. Then he realized the saloon had been fired deliberately, from the outside—all four walls of a building didn't start to burn at the same time of their own accord. Now he sniffed the faintly sweetish odor of coal oil and noted the thick smoke. The rifleman must have doused the oil around the foundation before heaving a rock through the window and calmly shooting to pieces a blanket that he had mistaken for Shorty Gibbs.

We got to get out of here, he thought to himself, before we're cut off on all sides. The women rattled down the steps, both of them wearing what seemed to be identical white-wrap-arounds. The Widow Courtney was still screaming. Goldie, with a fire of her own in her eyes, grabbed the torch in the middle of the floor and looked frantically for a place to throw it.

There wasn't any place. All four walls of the Plug Hat burned fiercely. The dry rawhide timber of the saloon burned with the intensity of twisted prairie grass in a monkey stove. Even as he watched, the walls were being consumed and fiery fingers were beginning to move along the naked rafters.

"Let's get out of here," he heard himself saying with unnatural calm. Let's have another drink. Let's shoot another game of pool. Let's get out of here before we're roasted like fat possums at Christmastime. He grabbed Goldie's arm and knocked the flaring torch out of her hand. "Here," he said, shoving the bullet-riddled blanket at the women, "hold this over you and follow me."

In a rage, Goldie shook free of his hold. "There's a pan of water behind the bar—we've got to put out this fire!"

"All the water in Gyp Creek wouldn't save this place now!" Already the saloon was boiling with oily black smoke and they began to cough. With every cough the knives gouged at Shorty's insides. He snarled at Goldie, and at the Widow Courtney who was still wringing her hands and screaming. "Don't waste your breath hollerin'," he snapped. "You're goin' to need it." He jerked Goldie away from the bar and covered the two women with the blanket. "We'll have to try the back door."

The front of the building was already a solid sheet of flames. The walls were beginning to buckle. Tongues of fire were already licking through the cracks in the back door. But the back wall was in better shape than the front. He shoved the women roughly toward the rear of the building.

It was searing hot now inside the saloon, hot enough to singe the stubble on Shorty's chin. The women stumbled blindly over tables and chairs. The roof was beginning to burn, raining live flame down on their heads.

At the door Shorty grasped the knob and jerked back a blistered hand. He tried the knob with his hand protected in his shirttail. The door was locked. "Where's the key!" he yelled at Goldie.

The saloon owner's head wagged beneath the blanket. "Upstairs in my room!"

Shorty swore in useless rage. He grabbed a chair and flailed at the burning door. Fiery splinters showered around them. The weakened door gave way and came loose from its hinges. Shorty pulled the women back as the door fell in. "And just about in time!" he started to say. But the words died unspoken. Facing them was not the dark, cool smelling out of doors that he had expected. Framed in the fiery doorway was a wall of glowing red-hot, sharp-edged steel. He stared with smoke tears, and maybe another kind as well, streaming down his face.

"What's the matter!" Goldie yelled from beneath the smoldering blanket.

Shorty didn't have the heart or time to tell her. Someone, and it wasn't hard to guess who—the rifleman—had thoughtfully stacked heavy prairie plows, grasshopper plows, in the doorway, guessing that Goldie and the Widow Courtney would make for the back alley when they saw the front of the building burning. Shorty Gibbs, of course, would already be dead, pegged to the table with rifle bullets. Yes sir, Shorty thought grimly, a mighty thoughtful bush-whacker!

There wasn't a chance of moving that mountain of red-hot steel out of the way before the walls collapsed and the roof fell in. "It ain't no good," he yelled to the women. "We'll have to go out the front way."

Goldie lifted the blanket and was too dismayed to do more than groan. Mrs. Courtney was even too terror-stricken to go on with her screaming. Shorty turned them around and guided them in the opposite direction.

It was useless. He couldn't get near enough to that wall of fire to kick the door down. He grabbed a table and tried to use it as a shield and battering ram, but the pain of lifting cut through him like a two-handed sword.

Pieces of the room began falling on them. All the oxygen in the building had gone to feed the fire, there was nothing left to breathe. Near the weakened area of the shattered window, the walls began to crumple. Shorty tried again to lift the table and fell into a fit of coughing. Then, as suddenly as a pistol shot, a piece of the wall exploded inward. For a moment there was black emptiness in the wall of fire. And out of the blackness came the huge form of Hoyt Tooms behind the empty fire barrel that he had used to batter his way inside.

"Where's the women at?" the marshal yelled at Shorty.

Shorty could only cough and point at the blanket where the women were huddled. "Don't go away," Tooms said dryly to Shorty. Then he grabbed Goldie under one arm and the Widow Courtney under the other and bulled his way back through the opening.

Drunkenly, Shorty shoved himself away from the table and immediately fell to his knees. Coughing, ignoring the knives, he pulled himself up again and staggered toward the opening. Tooms loomed hugely and caught him before he fell a second time. Shorty was agonizingly aware of being tucked under the marshal's thick arm and carried out like a sack of oats seconds before the front section of the roof came crashing down.

For some time after that he was aware only of pain and coughing. He found himself sitting against the raised plankwalk directly across the street from the now consumed Plug Hat. Goldie was washing his face with a piece of his own shirttail that she had dipped in a horse trough. "Here," she said, holding to his lips a tin cup that she had found in some unlikely place, filled with water from the same trough. He drank.

Finally the coughing stopped and the tearing pain eased. Beside him the Widow Courtney was staring blindly, pressing her white knuckles to her mouth. Shorty had the unpleasant feeling that if she took her hands away she would start screaming again.

He stared at the saloon. The roof had fallen in, and so had the front wall. As Shorty watched, the back walls collapsed and the whole building came down in a shower of live flame. He looked at Goldie, and she grinned and shrugged, as if it were nothing—unless you looked closely at her eyes.

"What's the difference?" she asked. "Runnin' a saloon in a one-horse town ain't nothin' to brag so loud about. I was ready to move out of Hardrow anyhow."

Sure, Shorty thought bitterly. Leave it to Shorty Gibbs to take care of his friends. Old Bohannan dead. And Goldie—a lifetime of work gone up in smoke and fire in less time than it took to tell about it. He didn't want to think of what it cost her, watching with a shrug and a grin as the Plug Hat burned to the ground.

"Where's Tooms at?" he asked after a while.

"Over with the others. Tryin' to keep the rest of the town from burning."

Shorty watched with cold unconcern as the citizens of Hardrow worked furiously to contain the fire. "Too bad there ain't a good stiff wind," he said. "They wouldn't have to go to all this bother."

Goldie said nothing. They made a strange and sorry sight, the three of them. Their clothing, such as it was, scorched and pitted with burns, their faces smudged with soot, their hair tousled and singed. But the worst thing was the feeling of emptiness that had for the moment seized them.

"Funny thing," Shorty said idly, as though he were commenting on the vagaries of Panhandle weather. "Funny thing about that stack of grasshopper plows in front of your back door. Where do you reckon they come from?"

"There's usually several at the blacksmith's. Left there to be sharpened."

Shorty grunted, not really giving a damn where they had come from. They had been there. That was the thing that counted. That bit of farsightedness on the part of the rifleman had very nearly got the two women burned alive, which was exactly what he had intended. For the moment Shorty ignored the more grisly aspects of this conclusion. For the moment he was interested only in why the assassin had planned it that way.

The best part of an hour must have passed with only a grunt or idle word passing between them. At last Tooms, his faded red nightshirt stuffed into his trousers, tramped wearily across the street. The fire was under control now. The Plug Hat had burned down to a heap of glowing coals, no danger to anyone, barring a sudden high wind.

"Looks like I ain't goin' to get any sleep at all, Gibbs, long as you stay in Hardrow."

Shorty looked at him but said nothing.

"Sorry about the Plug Hat, ma'am," the marshal said to Goldie. And the former saloon owner shrugged and grinned her grin and pulled the sexless wrapper a little tighter.

"It ain't much," Tooms said, "but you women better put up at my place rest of the night. Me and Gibbs can make do in the calaboose." Tooms knew that the citizenry of Hardrow were highly unlikely to take in the women—a saloon girl, and a living reminder of their own part in the lynching.

CHAPTER EIGHT

1

It was a one-room shack like most of the places in Hardrow, a door at one end, a window at the other, Indian style. It was surprisingly neat and orderly, as a lawman's thinking was supposed to be. The furnishings, except for a folding cot and a monkey stove with a stovepipe oven, consisted entirely of pine crates and boxes and vinegar kegs. The lone window was naked of curtains, but everything was scrupulously clean. The walls were papered with newspapers.

The thing that fascinated Shorty was the stovepipe oven. What did Tooms do with a thing like that?

The marshal draped a blanket over the window. "I never got around to puttin' a lock on the door, but you can pull in the latch string. And I'll leave this with you." He pressed a fully loaded .45 into Goldie's hand. "Don't wait to use this if anything comes up."

Somebody, he said, eyeing the narrow cot, would have to sleep on the floor. Goldie said they'd make out fine. Mrs. Courtney still looked stunned and said nothing. Tooms said well, he and Shorty wouldn't be far off, in case they were needed. Then he gathered a pair of blankets and the two men headed for the calaboose.

"Seems like I spend more time in the jailhouse than

anybody," Tooms said, throwing his blanket on the stone floor.

Shorty had already occupied the cell's only bunk. His silence was so intense that it seemed to ring. "All right," Tooms said wearily, "what is it?"

"That iron wall throwed up at Goldie's back door. It didn't get there by no accident."

"I figured," the marshal grunted. "When I first heard the shootin' and run out of the shack, I seen the fire run around the base of the buildin', like a primer of blastin' powder."

"Coal oil."

Tooms nodded. "That would do it. Anyhow, the front of the buildin' was already burnin', so I decided the back door would be the most likely place to bust in. I didn't notice the plows till then."

"You know why they was put there, don't you?"

"To keep you from gettin' out."

Shorty shook his head. "Not me. The women. The bushwhacker had already made sure of me—or thought he had—when he emptied his rifle into the pool table. But he couldn't get at the women with his rifle. Leastwise, he didn't have much chance of shootin' them while they slept, the way he figured to take care of me. So he thought up a way to start the saloon burnin' real fast. With all four walls doused in coal oil, the whole place would be on fire in a matter of seconds after he'd set torch to it. But the front part first of all. That would keep us away from the front door. Then we'd try the back way, and find it blocked.

By that time, he figured, it would be too late to try the front again. And he was right."

Tooms considered his rocky bed. "I don't know," he said at last. "I admit the fire don't look like much of an accident—but to deliberately set out to kill two women. Who would do a thing like that?"

"Tooms," Shorty said acidly, "I'm beginnin' to think you're too genteel for this job of marshalin'. Either that, or you're a plain fool. Or you're in the pay of the cowmen." He sensed immediately that he had gone too far. "But," he said grudgingly, "I guess it ain't that."

It was one of the few times in his life that Shorty Gibbs had backed away from something that he had talked himself into. "Well?" he said impatiently.

"It may be like you say," Tooms nodded. "And it may be that marshalin' ain't really my line of work. But the men I've knowed don't set out cold-blooded to kill women."

"You just have to know one. Somebody like Vance English, say."

"No." Tooms rejected the notion automatically.

"No," Shorty mimicked angrily. "You never believed that I seen Vance almost gun down Courtney's widow. It was the widow that somebody tried to trap in a burnin' building tonight."

2

Tooms, to Shorty's surprise, slept as lightly as he walked and talked. He did not rattle the calaboose bars with snoring, as Shorty had expected, and he did not throw his huge hulk about on the hard floor. He lay quietly, with his back to the stone wall, his .45 in his hand. Any slight sound from outside the jail, Shorty knew, would bring him instantly awake.

He put Tooms out of his mind. He ignored the many sharp pointed knives that dug at his insides, and the tight bindings that were beginning to itch. Well, he thought, you got it all figured, ain't you, Gibbs? All you got to do is walk up to the most powerful man in maybe five hundred miles of Hardrow and say, "Look here, English, your no-good son is a murderer and a woman killer to boot, so what do you aim to do about it?"

What English would very likely "do about it" was not too pleasant to contemplate.

Shortly before daylight Shorty hauled himself painfully out of the sagging bunk. Tooms was instantly awake.

"What do you think you're doin'?"

"I aim to get this thing unraveled, one way or another. I've been drygulched, burned out, and knocked around till I'm beginnin' to get tired of it. It ain't like I was in your boots, Tooms. My jurisdiction don't run out at the town limits."

"You never had any jurisdiction to begin with," Tooms said, "so just lay down and let me get some sleep."

"Remember what I told you about that old mutton puncher, the way he staked out one of the Spur hands? Well, maybe old Bohannan wasn't so far off the mark. Maybe that's the only language a cowman understands."

Tooms said in his old familiar purr, "We'll talk about it tomorrow."

"I'm through talkin'. The way things are goin' I'll be lucky just to be alive tomorrow."

The big marshal sat up on the stone floor. "Stay where you are, Gibbs."

Shorty pushed himself to his feet and stood wheezing and panting. He patted his waistband to make sure that he had that fancy .45 of Vance's. He felt for makings, but decided against smoking, the shape his lungs were in. "Good night, Tooms," he said, and limped out of the calaboose.

3

It was hard to keep track of the time. He didn't know if it was morning or afternoon until he checked with the sun. What I ought to of done, he thought, is brought along a bottle of whiskey to ease my ailments. Then he remembered that any whiskey that he might have put his hands on went up in flame when the Plug Hat burned.

He comforted himself with the knowledge that whiskey would only have made him thirsty, and he hadn't thought to bring any water. Worst of all, he hadn't brought any extra cartridges for the .45. He had only the five rounds that were always carried in a six-shot revolver, the hammer resting on an empty chamber for safety. At the moment he would rather have that extra round and take his chances on accidentally shooting himself in the groin.

He realized that his thoughts were wandering. Every time the pinto put hoof to the hard prairie the knives dug a little deeper. And as the knives dug he recalled certain savage details of the beating.

At last he brought the pinto to a stop and looked about him in surprise. Here he was back in that green valley where there was so much death, the dead animals rotting under the hot sun, pieces of the burned wagon scattered like black bones in the weeds.

There was a sudden heavy beating of wings as sluggish buzzards took flight. The stench was almost a visible thing, white and oily, rolling like ground fog up from the lush growth of the bottom.

What had brought him here? What instinct had turned him back toward such a place? Old man, he thought, if there was anything I could do, I'd do it— but I don't know what it would be.

Then, for a few bad seconds, he was sure that the fever had taken him. For just an instant he thought a

ghost had risen out of the ground, a ghost with an old
and weathered face beneath a battered hat. He shut his
eyes tightly and clamped his jaws. All right, he
thought. Take another look, Gibbs. Let's see if you
really are goin' loco.

He looked again and the figure was still there, but
not a ghost, a flesh and blood man on horseback,
riding horseback, riding slowly up the steep grade
from the creek. A man in his middle years, lean and
leathery, with tobacco stained mustaches drooping at
the corners of his mouth. He didn't look like old
Bohannan at all.

The man rode directly toward Shorty, watching him
with the intense concentration of a brand inspector.
His voice was as direct as his gaze.

"You got business here, mister, or do you just naturally take a fancy to such places?"

Shorty's nerve ends felt exposed and naked on the
surface of his skin. "I was about to ask you the same
thing."

The man smiled, but only with his mouth. "Was you
acquainted with the old man?"

"What old man?"

"The one that somebody buried down there in the
weeds. Name of Bohannan."

Somehow the stranger didn't have the look of a
cowman. "Who are you, and what have you got to do
with Bohannan?"

They studied each other like dogs meeting for the
first time. At last the stranger seemed to relax slightly.

"Dodd," he said. "Charlie Dodd. I ride for the Cattlemen's Association in Fort Worth."

Shorty wondered who was watching business in the home office; all the Association men seemed to be gathering in the Panhandle. "Is the Association interested in Bohannan?"

"It is now." He studied Shorty some more, even closer than before. "You wouldn't be the mail rider called Gibbs, would you?"

Shorty blinked. "Ex-mail rider. What about it?"

Charlie Dodd looked relieved. "I've been wanting to talk to you. Ralph Courtney was a pal of mine—I ain't got the whole story yet on how he died. I thought maybe you could help me."

Shorty looked at him and thought, Mister, you got a lot of disappointments ahead of you when you start askin' about Courtney.

"There's a story that a lynch mob got Courtney. Is it true?"

". . . Yes. But I can't prove it, and I don't think you'll find anybody that can. What did you mean by, *now* the Association had an interest in the old mutton puncher?"

Dodd felt in his shirt pocket and drew out what appeared to be a charred corner of a white envelope. "I found this in the ashes where the wagon had burned. It's part of an Association envelope; some of the printing is still on it. Must of been the old man that bushwhacked you and took the mail pouch and that report that Ralph Courtney had just mailed."

"I don't believe it," Shorty said bluntly. "How could an old mutton puncher know what was in that pouch?"

"Bohannan had been seen in Tascosa. Some of the boys claim they saw him followin' around after Courtney the day he mailed his report."

"For a shot of bar whiskey," Shorty said bitterly, "some of the boys would claim they seen Chief Big Tree sippin' tea with Little Phil Sheridan."

Charlie Dodd grinned faintly. "Maybe. But how do you explain this?" Indicating the charred paper.

Shorty shrugged. "Maybe he just picked it up. If I had been that bushwhacker, willin' to kill a mail rider to get my hands on Courtney's report, like as not I'd rip the envelope open on the spot to see if it was really what I wanted. The old man must of found it when he picked me up and took me to his wagon. Right where the bushwhacker had dropped it."

The Association man sighed. "I take it Bohannan must of been a pal of yours."

"He saved my hide once . . ." Shorty looked sharply at Dodd's lined face. "Do you know what was in that report of Courtney's?"

"If I knew that," Dodd said grimly, "I'd be ready to go back to Fort Worth."

"It comes to me," Shorty thought out loud, hugging his arms close to his aching ribs, "that we're lookin' for the same man. For different reasons, maybe, but the same man all the same. How would you like to hear a sad story about an ignorant mail rider that gets burned out and nigh murdered then turns down five hundred dollars cash money for a set of bruises and cracked ribs?"

4

"If this hunch of yours is wrong," Dodd said, "the Association will skin me alive and nail my hide to the company door."

"But if it's right we both get the man we're after." They hunkered in a patch of tall mullein, less than a hundred yards from the barred door of Hoyt Tooms' rock calaboose. But the place they had their eyes on was the marshal's shack.

"You sure that's where they are?" Dodd asked.

"That's where they was last time I seen them."

"Even if they are, how can you be sure our man'll come back again. Always a dangerous business, goin' back to correct a job you done wrong in the first place."

"But more dangerous if you *don't* go back."

They had left their horses in a wash and had slipped up to their position in the weed patch shortly before sundown. They had been waiting for almost an hour— waiting and watching the sluggish activity in Hardrow's street and alley. They had gone over everything many times, talking out their suspicions, comparing evidence, what little there was of it.

"Are you sure this marshal can be trusted?" Dodd asked.

Shorty shrugged painfully. "As much as you can trust any marshal."

They sank into a long period of silence as night came down on Hardrow. "There," Shorty said at last, when a crack of lamplight showed at the bottom of the shack's door. The door opened and Mrs. Courtney started out with a water bucket. But Goldie caught her and pushed her back. The former saloon owner went herself to a horse-trough pump, filled the bucket and took it back to the cabin.

"How much do you know about Mrs. Courtney?" Shorty asked.

Dodd shrugged. "Just a woman, like any other." After a moment he added, "Sometimes I used to wonder if she was the right one for Ralph Courtney."

"What made you wonder that?"

"I guess it was Ralph," Charlie Dodd said thoughtfully. "He took to his work like he'd been born to it. I mean, like the Association was the only outfit he'd thought about workin' for. He gave you the notion that any other kind of job would be beneath him, if you know what I mean."

Shorty knew. A lot of common cowhands, and even trail drivers, had the same kind of notion about their own jobs.

"Ralph Courtney was a good hand," Dodd went on. "He kept turnin' up ground after the rest of us gave a trail up as too cold to bother with. He was a bulldog; wouldn't let go before a case was finished to his own satisfaction."

"Even," Shorty prodded gently, "when a case was officially finished and he'd mailed in his reports?"

Dodd grinned faintly. "That was Courtney. I can see him goin' back over the trail just one more time, to make sure. The way he showed up in Hardrow that day with a flimsy story about returnin' a bad luck piece. His job was done. Him and the missus could of caught the next stage for Fort Worth, and that would of been the end of it. But he had that extra little bit of curiosity, and it got him killed."

"You sayin' that Mrs. Courtney ought to of married a store clerk or a bookkeeper instead of an Association detective?"

Dodd grunted, and for several seconds they were quiet. At last Shorty said, "I know how the Association is about keepin' family troubles to itself, but this ain't hardly just a family affair any more. There's been burn-outs, and killin', and the promise of more killin'. I'd like to know what brought Courtney to these parts in the first place, and just who he was investigatin'."

Dodd shot him a curious, slant-eyed look, but Shorty couldn't read it. It was possible that Dodd was on the verge of satisfying Shorty's curiosity. It was just as possible that the Association man was pegging him for a fool for even asking. Then, after due consideration, he said, "Maybe, when I find out a little more about it myself, I can tell you." Which, as Shorty knew, came close to saying nothing at all.

Shorty prodded his curiosity in another direction. "I don't recollect," he said blandly, "if I asked you about

Sam Milo, the Association man here in Hardrow."

Dodd smiled. "Milo's like a politician that nobody likes but everybody figures he's got powerful friends and they better not ruff his fur." He jabbed Indian-like with his chin. "Is that your marshal?"

Tooms had just rounded into the alley from the street. "That's him." Tooms scouted the back of the buildings and then returned to the calaboose and ducked inside. A few seconds passed. They saw Tooms strike a match and light a smoke. "Looks like we ain't the only ones keepin' an eye on the ladies tonight."

Time dragged. The Association man rubbed his chin and gazed thoughtfully at Shorty. He still wasn't sold on the idea that a killer was out to murder Courtney's widow. He was beginning to feel the fool, hiding out in the weeds while . . . Suddenly he sucked in his breath. "Did you see somethin'?"

Shorty squinted, aware that full darkness had settled on the town. Suddenly he grunted. A shadow flitted through the black-green weeds behind the calaboose.

A full minute passed in steely silence. Then another one. At last Dodd spoke. "Well, Gibbs, is it your killer?"

". . . Maybe." The shadow had dissolved in darkness and there was nothing to mark the spot where it had been. Shorty's mouth was suddenly dry. If it *was* the killer, he'd soon show himself. They were ready for him—the trap had been set and baited. And the bait was two women.

Dodd, with a grim smile, asked, "The women beginnin' to bother you, Gibbs?"

And what if they were? Shorty wondered with unfocused anger. It couldn't be helped. If the killer was Vance English, as Shorty suspected, he would have found the women, no matter where they were. Because, somehow, one of them had become a danger to him.

The Widow Courtney, in Shorty's mind, was little more than a notion, a vague memory without warmth or substance. But Goldie Vale was someone he knew, someone alive with laughter and humor and foolish generosity, and Shorty Gibbs was discovering that he didn't like the idea of risking Goldie's life on a hunch.

"Havin' a few second thoughts, Gibbs?" Dodd asked.

"If that's our man out there, I figure we ought to rush him now."

"All right," Dodd said. "Just point out where he is, exactly, and we'll rush him."

Pointing him out was impossible and Shorty knew it. He was out there somewhere, anywhere, in that sea of black mullein. "You know I can't pinpoint him. But if we let him know he's been spotted, he'll back off and let the women alone."

"Scare him away so he can come back another time when we don't expect him? You figure that's the best way to protect the women?"

Shorty knew that it wasn't, but that didn't make the

situation any more comfortable. Dodd said quietly, "I think I see. . . ."

And Shorty suddenly thought of something, but not until it was almost too late. "If I know my man, he won't be by hisself." He was thinking of Nate Corry, the faithful Spur foreman, heeling to Vance's command—or attacking like a well-trained wolfhound, and as dangerous. But by the time he had remembered Corry, the first prong of the attack had already got under way.

The door of the shack came open and lamplight sprayed out on the litter of the alley. A dark figure appeared in the doorway, tall, lithe, with hand-on-hip arrogance, and Shorty heard some idiot yelling at the top of his voice, "Goldie, get back! Shut the door!" He later realized that the idiot voice was his own. And anyway, it was too late for yelling, because the hidden rifle had already begun its killing fire.

A muzzle flash cut a long, bright gash in the darkness, and Charlie Dodd had wheeled instantly and was after it. Shorty wheeled in the opposite direction. The pearl-handled .45 was in his hand, ready to fire even before the next muzzle flash gave away the position of the second bushwhacker.

Dimly, Shorty was aware of other shooting. That would be Dodd, he guessed. And other yelling, and the angry rumbling voice of Hoyt Tooms sharply commanding the disturbance to stop. Then he felt the satisfying bucking of the .45 in his hand. He fired directly into a muzzle flash.

Suddenly it was over. The marshal's huge figure lurched in front of Shorty and lumbered toward the dark patch of weeds. Shorty started toward the shack but stopped when he saw both women in the doorway, apparently unhurt. Then he turned and saw Tooms kneeling in the weeds, a lighted match cupped in his hands.

Shorty walked toward him with queer woodenness.

Tooms looked up, his face drained of color. "He's dead—Lord help us. John English will burn this town to the ground and tromp the ashes into the dirt."

Just before the match flickered out Shorty glimpsed the strangely peaceful death mask that had a moment before been the face of Vance English.

5

The Widow Courtney clutched at the door facing of Tooms' shack, keening like a Comanche squaw. The sound roared just within the limits of Shorty's consciousness as he straightened and looked at Tooms. "What about the other rifleman?" It was a little late to worry about Vance.

"I ain't sure," the marshal said tightly. "I think your partner dropped him." His tone hardened. "Just where is your partner? And who is he?"

"Association man," Shorty heard himself saying vacantly, "name of Dodd." He raised his voice and shouted at the darkness. "Charlie Dodd!"

The whiplike figure raised up out of the weeds. "This one's hurt, Gibbs. Better see if you can raise a doctor."

Tooms groaned. The nearest thing to a doctor was Murph Hogan, wagon yard hostler and part-time vet. "Nate Corry?" the marshal asked.

Shorty grunted. "Must be. John English has kept him trailin' after Vance ever since this trouble started."

The big cat was no longer purring. It was snarling, and it was dangerous. "Killin' John English's only boy, and maybe his foreman, to boot. It might of been a mercy if you'd set fire to the town while you was at it. That's better than we're apt to get at the hands of the Spur bunch."

Shorty broke through his shell of numbness and found anger. "Don't preach to me, Tooms. You saw what happened. They deliberately set out to kill the women—what did you expect me to do!"

The marshall swelled in anger, then seemed to shrink in frustration. "All right," he said. "We'll have to make the best of it." He turned to Goldie Vale who was coming toward them from the shack.

Goldie gazed at the dark dead figure of Vance English. "I feel like I ought to hate him. But it would be like hating a stump or a fence post, wouldn't it? I'd give a pretty, if I had one, to know what made him want to kill me."

"It was the widow," Shorty said. "At least I think it was. But I don't know why—not yet."

Charlie Dodd called again. "Gibbs, you got anybody started after the doctor?"

A few cautious townsmen were gathering anxiously around the shack. Tooms yelled for them to get on about their business, but they only backed out of the light and watched.

Shorty asked quietly, "Does anybody know if any Spur hands was in town?"

As the last word was spoken—or so it seemed—they heard the clatter of hoofs heading away from Hardrow. The big marshal heaved a long sigh. "There ain't now. John English will have the word within an hour, if that rider don't kill his horse tryin' to make it sooner."

They left Vance where he lay, quartered across the slant of light from the shack, and made for the slender figure of Charlie Dodd. Tooms struck another match, glanced harshly at the Association man's face, then turned the flickering light on the man in the weeds. It was Corry, all right, with a hole in his thigh and most of his blood, so it seemed on the ground.

"Anybody know him?" Dodd asked with businesslike crispness.

"Nate Corry," Tooms said grimly. "John English's foreman. The other one's the old man's boy. Vance. He's dead."

Dodd's eyes widened, and his lips pursed, as if to whistle. "There'll be some hell raised in Fort Worth," he murmured to himself. "And some fresh hides pegged out to dry—most likely mine'll be the first."

"Not if John English gets to you first," Shorty told him.

"Goddamn you all!" Corry grated. "Do you aim to just stand there and watch me bleed to death? Why don't you put a bullet in my throat and end it fast!"

Moving with queer reluctance, as if they hated to disturb this sudden, unnatural silence that passed for the moment as peace, Tooms and Dodd lifted the foreman and carried him to the shack. Shorty followed with Goldie Vale. Corry gritted his teeth in pain and clammy sweat broke out on his face when they stretched him out on the floor. But the expression of pain touched no sympathy in Shorty Gibbs; pain was his constant companion and had been for more hours than he liked to remember.

At least, Shorty thought to himself, the Widow Courtney had stopped her keening. Be grateful for small favors. She was pressing back against the door frame, staring with saucer eyes at Corry's twisted face. The foreman looked at her, stared at her for the best part of a minute, unblinking, coldly. Then, amazingly, he laughed.

It crossed Shorty's mind that it would be mighty interesting if he could somehow look inside Corry's head. The same sort of thought had also occurred to Tooms and Dodd. But then the widow uttered a thin, mouselike little sound and wrenched away from his gaze.

With a return of anger, Corry snarled, "Goddamn you, Tooms, did you tote me all the way to your shack just to watch me bleed on your floor?"

With an air of resignation, Goldie Vale began ripping up another bedsheet. "Somebody build a fire," she said, "and put some water on to heat."

CHAPTER NINE

1

Charlie Dodd was saying dryly, "I don't guess there's any use settin' and waitin' and hopin' that a county judge and a jury will get all this straightened out in good time."

And Tooms said just as dryly, "No use at all."

"How far is it to Spur headquarters?"

"Twenty miles, maybe, by wagon track. Considerable shorter if you don't mind dogtowns and cut banks."

"Two hours, I'd say," Dodd mused, "and we can expect company." He studied Tooms' wide worried face. "Don't you think we ought to move the women out of the line of fire?"

Shorty, sitting bolt upright on the bunk, thinking of his own pain, absently watched the marshal's face grow hot. "That's a fine idea. Except there ain't no place we could send them, short of Tascosa. Maybe you ain't heard, but the widow's rig come down with a busted axle, and her animal's down with the colic. Maybe Goldie could horseback it that far, but not the widow."

"There must be rent rigs."

Tooms shook his head. "Not for anybody runnin' from John English. And especially not tonight."

"What do you aim to do?"

"Set and wait." Tooms put some of his pent-up savagery into a slit of a grin. "Unless you got a better notion."

The three men had gathered in the rock calaboose to make plans for avoiding a head-on collision with the cowmen, if that was possible. So far the talk had gone in circles, getting them nowhere. Because, Shorty thought to himself, there was nowhere for them to go. No escape. A showdown with English was what he had wanted, and a showdown was what he would soon be getting.

"Sam Milo," Shorty said abruptly, and the other two faces turned to look at him in the flickering light of a tallow candle. "Seems like he's the weakest link in the English chain . . ."

Charlie Dodd had read his thoughts. "If I ever get back to Fort Worth I can get him fired, but he ain't likely to listen to me now. Even if I knew where he was and could talk to him. He's in too deep."

"Too deep in what? Maybe he hasn't got mixed up in murder yet. But he must of knowed somethin' about Courtney's investigation."

Tooms and Dodd lost interest. The key word to every suggestion had been "if" and it had only led them around in more circles. They could stand and fight, but they couldn't hope to win against the cowmen. On the other hand, they couldn't run, because the women—Mrs. Courtney, anyway—had no way to travel.

"Can't we get some of the townsmen to pitch in with us?" Dodd asked.

Tooms laugh harshly. That laugh said everything he had to say about the citizens of Hardrow.

"Maybe we do have one chance," Shorty said slowly. "We'll have to send somebody for help."

Tooms snorted in disgust. "I gave you credit for more sense, Gibbs. A day's ride to Tascosa, a day's ride back, and you couldn't find anybody to take a hand in this trouble, anyhow. Even if you did, it wouldn't do any good. John English would be finished with us long before."

"Not Tascosa," Shorty said. "The only place we're likely to get any help is at Emery Straiter's Double E headquarters, and at Paul Maston's Singletree."

An expression of even greater disbelief flitted across the marshal's face. "You're loco, Gibbs. Maston and Straiter throwin' in with us, against John English?"

But Charlie Dodd was surprisingly quiet. "Like Gibbs says, maybe it's the only chance we've got."

"You're *both* loco!"

"This has been English trouble right from the beginnin'," Shorty continued, as if he had never been interrupted. "Maston and Straiter went along with it because they was all cowmen, but they never took the interest in it that English did."

"That don't mean they're about to *turn* on English." Then they both looked at Charlie Dodd.

The Association man had retreated to the privacy of his own thoughts. His eyes took on a curious glaze as

166

he stared into the flickering light. "Gents," he said at last, "nobody knowed what was in that report of Ralph Courtney's but Ralph hisself, and he ain't in no way to talk. And the ones responsible for stealin' the reports, of course, and they ain't talkin', either. But I do know it was a mighty important matter that concerned every cowman in Texas, not just a handful of top dogs up here in the Panhandle. As maybe you've heard, there's talk down in Austin of rewritin' the free range laws."

"There's always talk where there's politicians," Tooms said.

"This is somethin' more'n just talk. Folks don't look to the cow any more as their only salvation. It hurts me some to say it, but the cowman ain't God any more. A dirt farmer's vote counts just as much as the vote of John English . . ."

Tooms snapped impatiently. "What's all this got to do with the stew we're in?"

"Just that the cowman all of a sudden finds hisself in deep water and he ain't right sure how good he is at swimmin'. The farmers are hollerin' for free land. They're startin' to put pressure on the politicians to bust up the free range. You know what that would mean to the big ranches. It would mean ruin."

"I still don't see . . ." Tooms started. But then, quite suddenly, he did see. "If the Spur outfit threatens to get the whole cow business in Dutch, Straiter and Maston might just be forced to team up against English."

Dodd grunted. "English may be the biggest cowman hereabouts, but that don't mean that Straiter and Maston would let him sink them without a fight."

"Can we convince them that English is tryin' to sink them?"

"I might," Dodd said. "They might put some stock in what I say because I'm with the Association."

Shorty was doing some fast figuring, allowing two hours for a runner to reach Singletree headquarters, and another hour for him to get to the Double E. Throw in another hour for steady talk and hard persuasion—and that, Shorty thought, was being optimistic. Any way you took it, and even if you were willing to believe that Straiter and Maston would swallow Dodd's story, it would still be daylight at the very earliest that they could expect any kind of help. And in about one hour John English and his crew would land on Hardrow with murder in their hearts.

Shorty and Tooms considered the scheme in gloomy silence. "It won't work," Tooms said at last. "Straiter and Maston won't turn against their own."

But even wolves, Shorty knew, turned against their own when one went mad and endangered the pack. "Anyhow," Tooms argued, "me and Gibbs couldn't hold out all night. Not against the whole Spur outfit. And with two women on our hands." The marshal had been doing some figuring of his own.

Dodd shrugged. "You got a better notion, Marshal?"

The candle guttered and went out—which, Shorty thought, was just as well, for the look of defeat was mirrored in their faces. He got painfully to his feet and limped to the open door of the calaboose. "If we was to pile somethin' here in front of the door," he thought aloud, "some sacks of feed, maybe, we might be able to fort up for quite a spell."

Tooms thought about it, and after a moment groaned to himself. "It ain't like we had any choice in the matter. You know how to find Singletree and Double E?" he asked Dodd.

"I can find them. Mind you, I can't guarantee to bring back any help—it's just a notion."

Shorty wished he knew more about that report of Courtney's; it might tell him how much leverage they could use on Straiter and Maston. This here's goin' to be a mighty sorry way to cash in, he thought grimly, if this scheme fails to work. Nothin' much worse then gettin' your fool self killed with a head full of unanswered questions.

2

Hardrow was a ghost town with ghostly sounds faintly stirring the uneasy air. Marshal Hoyt Tooms placed a heavy sack of shelled corn in front of the calaboose door, then stood for a moment, wiping his face, listening. "They're pullin' out," he said at last.

"I heard," Shorty grunted. He was attempting to knock a hole in the side of the rock wall, but he couldn't lift the heavy sledge that Tooms had brought from Boss O'Dell's general store. He rested against the side of the wall, panting, hugging his bandaged ribs.

"Scatterin' like a tromped-on bed of red ants," the marshal said in a tone of grim wonder.

"They seen what happened to Vance. They know trouble's on the way. And they know John English." If I wasn't so bullheaded, Shorty thought, I'd be pullin' out with them.

"Can you shoot a rifle?" Tooms asked.

Shorty tried unsuccessfully to shoulder an imaginary rifle. "I don't think so."

"Take this." Tooms handed him his own .45 and some cartridges. "That'll give you two handguns. I'll get your saddle gun out of your ridin' rig and use it as a spare."

"How're the women doin'?"

The marshal gave his face another wipe and pocketed the bandanna. "Goldie's lookin' after Nate Corry. The widow's nigh scared to death. And with reason, maybe, if English figures she knows what was in that report of her husband's."

"I wonder if she does," Shorty said, almost to himself.

Tooms headed back to O'Dell's store where, in a very unlawman-like way, he had broken down the back door, and was soon returning with another heavy sack of feed.

"I figured," Shorty said, "if we was to knock loopholes in these two walls we'd have a better chance of seein' what was goin' on. But I can't lift the sledge."

With machine-like efficiency, Tooms took the big hammer and pounded sandstone rocks loose from their beds of grainy mortar. In a matter of minutes he had opened holes big enough to shoot through on either side of the calaboose. The new openings, with the doorway and the small barred window, gave them a reasonably good field of fire on all four sides.

"There's one more thing," Shorty said when Tooms had finished with the sledge. "These rived shingles and pine rafters might do good work against rain and hail, but how'd they do against fire, if somebody thought to fling a coal-oil torch up there?"

The marshal could see the danger that a dry wood roof presented. He tramped off into the darkness and soon returned with Shorty's pinto and a thick coil of lariat. He dabbed a loop on a gable joint and, with some help from the pinto, brought the roof crashing to the ground.

Tooms stood looking at the ruins of what had recently been a reasonably presentable calaboose. He glanced at Shorty, but kept his thoughts silent. He studied his sacked corn breastworks and decided that it was high enough. "Guess I might as well go get the women."

"And Corry?"

"Him, too. Goin' to make it a mite crowded in here." The men inspected their makeshift fort from the out-side, circling it slowly, Shorty grunting painfully with every step. "I don't guess it's anything a general would be too proud of," Tooms said, "but it's about as good as we can make it."

Just how good it was would depend on English and how much determination he had, and how many men. The old cowman, they knew, would very likely have plenty of both. Shorty sat stiffly erect on the calaboose bunk while Tooms went after the women. What we need, he thought gloomily, is two good sharpshooters at them loopholes.

What they needed was more like a company of infantry, and maybe a Gatling gun. What they needed was a drastic change in luck. Shorty built a smoke and hung it in the corner of his mouth unlighted. What they needed was a lot of faith in Charlie Dodd's powers of persuasion, just in case Dodd reached Straiter and Maston before blundering into English men. Assuming of course, that his horse hadn't already stepped into a doghole or run off a cut bank, which, everything considered, was a lot of assuming.

What they *didn't* need was two women and one of the wounded enemy underfoot.

Over the sacks of corn he watched Tooms coming across the dark alley with the women. Hands on hips, Goldie Vale stood for a moment regarding the ruined jail. "Well," she said dryly, "I hope it don't rain."

Tooms explained briefly that pulling the roof down had been a safety measure, but the explanation was wasted on the women. Goldie already knew the reasons—she had only to sniff the night air and smell the charred rubble of what had once been her saloon; no one had to explain to her about dry timber and coal oil and fire. Mrs. Courtney didn't understand a word that had been said. She was nearly paralyzed with fear. She could only wring her hands and stare blindly at the rock walls.

"Well . . ." Tooms left his explanation dangling. "I'll go after Corry. You ladies make yourselves comfortable as you can. Likely we've got a long wait ahead of us."

A late moon had drifted unnoticed into the dark sky. The Widow Courtney cowered into a dark corner of the jail.

"How long's she been like this?" Shorty asked uneasily.

Goldie shrugged. "Ever since she realized Vance English was dead and that the old man would soon be landin' on Hardrow, thirstin' for blood. I guess you know the town's about empty except for the four of us, and Corry."

"I know."

"Funny thing," Goldie said wonderingly. "Once I saw a feed barn catch fire, and it was somethin' to give you nightmares, the way the horses screamed when the fire got too high and the hostlers couldn't get them out. There was a big crowd, a bucket gang and everybody givin' advice and yellin'—but the thing I remember most was the rats leavin' the barn, makin' little scurryin' sounds, escapin' the fire almost without a notice while fine-blooded horses were trapped and died. Well, that's what I thought about tonight, when the good folks of Hardrow started to scamper. They're

out there now." She made an aimless gesture. "Hidin'
in gullies and washes, waitin' and watchin', I guess,
while better men . . ."

She had started to say, "While better men prepared
to die."

"Rats ain't the only animals that run from a fire.
Folks do it too, if they're smart. Look," he said suddenly, "my pinto's in pretty good shape. And Tooms'
horse is still in the livery barn, if somebody hasn't
turned him out. Why don't you and the widow . . . ?"

Goldie shook her head. "The widow wouldn't last
ten minutes on horseback. Anyhow, I ain't ready just
yet to leave Hardrow. There's the little matter of my
saloon—I figure somebody's got to settle for that, one
way or the other." Did she grin, or was it Shorty's
imagination? "You ain't the only one that can be bullheaded, you know."

Tooms was returning from the shack, half-carrying
the hopping, cursing Nate Corry. A sudden silence
made itself felt as the marshal ushered the wounded
foreman around the barrier of grain sacks.

None too gently, Tooms forced Corry down to the
floor. "Just set there," he told the foreman, "and keep
quiet and out of the way."

"Goddammit!" Corry winced as he straightened out
his wounded leg.

"And watch your tongue," Tooms warned coldly,
"when you're in the company of ladies."

Pale light fell on the foreman's drawn face. He lay
back against the sacks of corn. With visible effort he

174

drove his anger to the back of his mind. "Tooms," he said, "you're a bigger fool than I thought if you try to stand off John English. You and Gibbs won't last five minutes."

"We'll last a little longer than that," Tooms said.

"Five minutes or an hour, what good's it goin' to do?"

The marshal merely smiled. The Widow Courtney cowered deeper into her corner. "Wait a minute . . ." Corry scowled. "There was three of you when the shootin' started. What happened to your pal? He pull out on you, like all the others?"

Shorty got slowly to his feet. "Our pal," he said softly, "is an Association man. And he didn't pull out, he's gone for help."

Corry made a sound of surprise. And so—from her dark corner—did the widow. The marshal turned with a look of concern. "What is it, Mrs. Courtney?"

"Nothing!" She sounded as if she were trying to push herself through the rock wall.

Corry's face was blank for a moment. Then, abruptly, he laughed. "We been doin' some wonderin' about you, Mrs. Courtney," the foreman said, his tone dripping with sarcasm. "Vance claimed the old man was wastin' his time and money on you. But that was Vance. Most of the time he was wrong."

"No," the Widow Courtney murmured, as she might have spoken the word in her sleep while dreaming. "No . . . No . . ."

Corry laughed again. Tooms suddenly exploded. "What's goin' on here!"

"I was about to tell you, Marshal." The foreman grinned with not the faintest trace of humor. "Like I was sayin', when John English gets you pegged, there's no mistake about it. Vance, as usual, had Courtney's widow pegged all wrong. Vance knowed just one way to settle a misunderstandin', and that was with a gun."

"From ambush?" Shorty asked coldly.

Corry grinned with false good humor. "Well, not always. He would of faced up to the widow, I guess. But of course she wasn't in no way to shoot back."

"That the day Mrs. Courtney first come to Hardrow—out on the Tascosa road?"

Corry hesitated, looking from Shorty to the marshal. "Boys," he said at last, "seems like you've got a lot of questions, and maybe I've got some answers. It comes to me that we might be able to strike a bargain."

"No bargain," Shorty said.

But Tooms asked quietly. "What's on your mind, Corry?"

"For one thing, I want to be let out of this calaboose before English and his crew get here. He'll knock this jail down a rock at a time, if he has to, to get at the ones that killed Vance. When that time comes I want to be somewheres else . . ."

He waited. "Well," Tooms said thoughtfully, "you ain't in any way to doin' much fightin', I guess. What've you got to trade for a ticket out of here?"

The foreman shook his head in mock sadness. "Tooms, I thought you had better sense. Tacklin' a

176

cowman in his own front yard. Take a piece of free advice, boys, and make a run for it. Not that it'll save your scalp. But at least make English work a little harder to take it."

"Is that all you got to trade?"

Corry winced as he moved his wounded leg. For one long moment he gazed into the dark corner where the Widow Courtney cowered. "Mrs. Courtney," he said conversationally. "Vance English had kind of a theory about you. He figured if a-body wasn't worth livin', then they might as well be dead. Of course he never quite seen hisself in the same light as he seen others. Anyhow, right from the beginnin' Vance was for killin' you—he would of done it that day on the road if it hadn't been for Gibbs . . ."

He looked up at Shorty and grinned. "There wouldn't nobody believe you, would they? Vance had that figured too. In some ways he was smart, maybe even smarter than his old man." He shifted his attention back to the dark corner. "Vance was a great one for sizin' people up, whether he knew anything about them or not. He had you pegged as a nagger, Mrs. Courtney. A naggin' wife that trailed after her husband and got in his way and did her best to keep him from doin' the only thing in the world he was good at, bein' an Association man. It didn't count to Vance that you was a woman. He pegged you as no-account and figured it would be better for everybody if he just shot you. Mrs. Courtney," Corry asked mildly, "was Vance so very far off the mark, after all?"

Tooms reared up in righteous indignation. "I won't stand for that kind of talk, no matter if you have got a bullet in your leg!"

The foreman shrugged. "You asked what I had to trade. Well, I'm tellin' you, but I'll have to do it my own way, and it'll take a little time."

Shorty said impatiently, "Let him talk."

Corry lay back against the grain sacks and closed his eyes. Sweat rolled down his face as he readjusted his leg. "Well," he went on, "the old man nigh blowed up when he heard what Vance nearly pulled off back on the Tascosa road that day. John English claimed there'd already been too much killin'. Folks was startin' to talk, he said. Big folks in important places. These is touchy times. The cowman ain't king o' the hill, like in the old days. There is times when a man, even John English, has to watch his step."

Shorty made a growling sound in his throat. "We don't give a damn what John English *thinks*."

"You ought to," Corry said. He looked up at their pale faces. "Anyhow," he said, "the old man was dead set against more killin'. Which is why you're still alive, Gibbs. It's also why," he added blandly, "the Widow Courtney all of a sudden got to be a rich woman."

They stared at him, the sense of his words going over their heads. "But you folks didn't know about her bein' rich, did you? Why don't you show them, Mrs. Courtney?"

She crowded even deeper into the shadows.

All eyes turned to look at the thin, dark figure of

panic. "You know what he's talkin' about, Mrs. Courtney?" Tooms asked in a worried tone.

"Sure she does," Corry said with a new note of smugness. "Five hundred dollars in double eagles, ain't it, ma'am? I seen John English count it out and put it in the buckskin pouch along with the note. Do you still have that note, Mrs. Courtney?"

"No!" As if it was the only word she knew.

"You didn't lose the note, did you? Or maybe throw it away?"

"No!" There was cornered wildness in that single syllable. "I mean—I don't know about any note!"

"There was a note, ma'am. I saw John English write it and put it in with the money. And I was the one that scouted the saloon that mornin' to make sure that you was upstairs by yourself. Then I pitched the pouch through the upstairs window where you'd be sure to find it."

"I . . . I never found any pouch."

"Well, now." Corry turned to Goldie. "Did you find it, Goldie? You or the widow, one of you must of found it."

It occurred to Shorty that Corry was dragging out the pain. There was something in the foreman that enjoyed seeing others squirm.

Goldie turned to Mrs. Courtney, wanting to speak quietly, reassuringly, but when the words came out they were barbed with suspicions. "Was there a pouch? Did you find it?"

Shorty already knew the answer. It was in the smugness of Corry's tone. But most of all it was in that remembered call that he had paid on the widow, at her request. It had been then, so suddenly and for no apparent reason, that she had decided to drop the search for the mob leader.

Mrs. Courtney said nothing. She was beaten, defeated. She knew what they were thinking of her— that she had accepted profit from her husband's murder. She must have seen it in their coldly staring eyes, felt it in the arid silence. Only her panic kept her from collapsing.

Tooms was the first to turn back to Corry, and his voice was smooth and soft, a quiet thunder from far away. "Is that all?"

"Just about. Of course she's lyin' about the money— she's got it. But most likely she got rid of the note. Not a comfortin' thing to have around, I guess. But five hundred dollars is a lot of money. And your husband's a long time dead, ain't that right, Mrs. Courtney? What difference will it make to him?"

"That's enough," Tooms snapped, and Corry heard the danger there and was silent.

Shorty asked in a voice that he hardly recognized, "So it was Vance all along that got the lynch mob together and broke him out of jail."

"Sure, it was Vance." Corry sighed, thinking what a relief it was not to have the responsibility of looking after John English's spoiled pup any more.

"You knowed it all the time," Shorty accused Tooms.

Tooms came erect. His flat face seemed to glow in the dark. "What I know don't mean a thing. It's what I can prove that counts in a court of law."

Corry grinned at them. Shorty fixed his attention on the foreman.

"Why did Courtney have to die? Why was that so important to Vance?"

Corry looked as if he was about to speak, then changed his mind. "I told you all I know."

Shorty shook his head. "You told us that Vance led the lynch mob—but Vance ain't in any shape to answer for it. And you say the widow took English's money to set quiet and not make trouble. And maybe she did. But just how much trouble could one woman make?"

"Plenty, if she knows what was in that report . . ." Corry broke off abruptly, realizing that he was talking too much.

But Shorty jumped on his last word. "That report! I think the mud's beginnin' to settle. Things are gettin' a little clearer. That report dealt with Vance, didn't it? Anybody that knowed about it was in a way to get him in a lot of trouble. That explains why he arranged to get Courtney hung and tried to kill his widow. John English wanted to cover up for Vance, but was against stirrin' up more dust with more killin' . . ." The theory was all right as far as it went, but it still didn't fully explain why English had suddenly taken a dislike to gunplay. "Exactly what was in that report?"

"I never asked," Corry said blandly, "and never heard anybody say."

Shorty flushed and turned to Mrs. Courtney. "Ma'am . . ."

Corry laughed derisively. "You won't get anything out of her, Gibbs. John English might want his gold back if she ever started talkin'." The foreman squinted up at them in obvious bewilderment. "Don't it mean nothin' to you folks that this woman would agree to English's proposition, swappin' justice for gold?"

"I wouldn't," Tooms purred, "talk about justice, if I was you, Corry."

The foreman heard the danger in that smooth voice but preferred to shrug it off. "A woman like that ain't worth dyin' for, Gibbs. You and Goldie and Tooms could just saddle up and light out of here. You might even have a chance of out runnin' English, without that woman to look after."

"Just shut up a while," Shorty said wearily.

"Is that all you figure to trade?" Tooms asked.

"I've just showed how you don't have to stay here and get your fool selves killed on that woman's account. Don't that mean anything to you?"

"No," the marshal said bluntly, then went to one of the jagged loopholes and gazed out at the silent night.

"You don't aim to keep me here out of pure cussedness, do you?" Corry hadn't expected this turn of events; he was beginning to be concerned.

In a tone so flat that it bordered on indifference, Shorty asked, "Corry, tell me somethin'—how come you and Vance had to kill that old mutton puncher, Bohannan?"

It was a wild shot, but it caught the foreman by surprise. He sat suddenly erect and gasped as pain took his breath away. That moment of pain brought him time enough to recover from his surprise. "What mutton puncher?"

"Give me a hand," Shorty snarled to Tooms. "Let's get him out of here."

CHAPTER TEN

1

Shorty and Tooms left the foreman on the plankwalk in front of O'Dell's store and returned to the calaboose. "Maybe that was a mistake," Shorty worried. "He may be out of the fight, but he can still talk. And I don't like to think what kind of story he'll be tellin' that old cowman."

"It won't be any worse than English has already told hisself. Anyhow, I'd had all of Corry I could take." They circled the charred remains of the Plug Hat Saloon and slanted toward the jail.

Shorty said, "I'd liked it better if Corry hadn't talked so much about the widow."

Tooms grunted. "She wasn't in no pretty spot—her husband dead, throwed out on her own with nobody to depend on. And no money, if I know anything about range detectives." He slowed almost to a stop and spoke softly. "So don't be too fast to judge her, Gibbs."

2

A dime-sized moon shone weakly in the eastern sky. A strained silence had settled over the group in the

184

makeshift fort. Tooms lounged at one of the loopholes watching the street. Shorty sat bolt upright on the bunk concentrating on breathing as shallowly as possible and trying to ignore the pain. Goldie sat beside him in moody silence. The Widow Courtney huddled in her corner, her face turned from the others.

"You ought to of lit out of here when you had the chance," Shorty said at last, glancing at Goldie.

The former saloon owner made an unlady-like sound and sank deeper into her own thoughts.

What, Shorty asked himself from time to time, am I doin' here anyhow? This wasn't his town any more. What did he care if English pulled it down and kicked it to pieces? What difference could it make to Shorty Gibbs if an overcurious range detective had got himself strung up by a lynch mob? The solid citizenry of Hardrow didn't seem to care. Why should he?

The plain fact was he was in no shape to make a run for it. For Shorty Gibbs it was stand and face English, or burrow in some nearby gully and wait for them to flush him out. So don't start feelin' like no hero, he told himself. You're here for the same reason as the others—you don't really have any say-so in the matter.

Tooms? Well, the marshal was here because it was his job. And Goldie was here because she was so red-headed stubborn that she couldn't pull stakes without hitting back at somebody for burning her saloon. The widow had no rig, and couldn't ride horseback, and she couldn't bring herself to break away from the only people in town foolish enough to befriend her.

Some bunch of heroes, Shorty thought wryly.

Still, he knew that it wasn't quite that simple. Nothing was stopping Tooms from jerking that badge off his vest. And what held Goldie was something more than blind stubbornness. No matter what the widow had done, Goldie had no intention of throwing her to English's wolves.

"First light," Tooms said thoughtfully, indicating a watered milk paleness along the eastern horizon. But it was the false dawn that always appeared on the prairie—the real dawn would come several minutes later.

"Wonder where Dodd is by now?" Goldie wondered out loud.

Shorty shrugged. Tooms rested his rifle in the jagged loophole. "Town's quiet as a graveyeard." Which, as far as Shorty Gibbs was concerned, was a might poor way of stating it. "We can be expectin' the Spur crew anytime now, if I know English."

The real dawn arrived with appalling suddenness, the sterile light revealing the prairie in the needle-sharp detail of a steel etching. Shorty began to have more doubts about Nate Corry. The foreman, left where he could give English his side of the story as soon as the Spur bunch hit town, was not going to make things any easier. Still, he was just as glad to have the foreman out of sight.

Tooms stood a little straighter. "You hear anything?"

Shorty shook his head.

The marshal scowled, fiercely attentive, his head cocked like some huge bird on the verge of sudden flight. Goldie Vale was saying, "Mrs. Courtney, why don't you sit over here? You must be near dead."

The widow, her face turned down, her eyes focused on the stone floor, shook her head. "All night long I've been thinkin', and thinkin', tryin' to think of a way to explain why I did what I did. But there just isn't any way . . ."

"Forget it," Goldie said, the natural brassiness of her voice muted. "You had a bad time; there ain't none of us here blamin' you for anything."

But Mrs. Courtney went on in the same dead tone. "I was scared, I guess. More scared than I've ever been before. Not because my life was in danger—I guess I never actually believed that. I loved my husband—at least I think I did—but when I learned that he was dead . . ." She glanced up in dull pain. "Even then, it wasn't grief I felt, but fear. Fear of bein' left alone. Nowhere to go, nobody to take me in. No money to get me started somewhere else . . ."

Shorty turned toward her, an old interest rekindled. "Mrs. Courtney, you might be in a way to help us, if you wanted to."

Goldie flared. "This ain't the time to go into that!"

"There'll never be a better time," Shorty said grimly. "How about it, Mrs. Courtney? We know now that Vance English led the mob that broke your husband out of jail and strung him up." He was deliberately crude and cruel, hoping to shock her back to

187

reality. Tooms wheeled and said angrily, "Look here, Gibbs!" But Shorty pushed on, knowing that he had to act now while the urge to talk was upon her.

"Vance English," he repeated. "Mrs. Courtney, do you know why Vance had to kill your husband?"

She stared at him with watery eyes. ". . . Had to kill Ralph?"

"Yes ma'am. It wasn't no accident that Vance got that mob together, like it wasn't no accident that he aimed to kill you in the fire."

Goldie glanced sharply at the two of them. "I was in that fire too. Vance didn't have any reason to kill me."

"Maybe he did. He knew that Courtney had told his wife about it, and that made her as dangerous to him as Courtney hisself. Then, since she was stayin' at your place, she might of told you . . ."

Goldie gazed at him steadily. "That's loco," she said at last.

"So was Vance, maybe. On the edge of it, anyhow, because of what Courtney knew about him."

With a few words he had built a chill logic that settled on them with the clamminess of a shroud. "What was in that report, Mrs. Courtney?"

"I don't know," she said in a thin voice. "But I'm sure there was nothing in it about Vance English."

"How can you be sure?"

"My husband would have told me. He never kept secrets from me."

"You said before that your husband never discussed Association business with you. Which is it, Mrs.

Courtney? Did he have something on Vance or didn't he?"

"Take it easy, Gibbs," Tooms was saying in a dark velvet voice.

But Shorty continued to push, his tone taking on an edge of scorn. "If you know somethin', there's just a chance that we can get English to listen before he pulls this calaboose down on our heads. Of course," he added dryly, "there's the chance, too, now that his boy's dead, he might not figure that your silence is so valuable."

Her face in that whey-ey light was as colorless as leaf tallow. She looked frail and old and sick, but none of it at that moment touched Shorty Gibbs. "Is that it, Mrs. Courtney? Are you so scared of losin' that money that you'll stand there and say nothin', putting your own life on the line, as well as ours?" Breathing was difficult and painful—he paused for a moment, breathing shallowly through his mouth. "Five hundred gold," he continued. "That's what Corry said. Does it mean so much to you? I wonder if your husband meant as much when he was alive."

"Gibbs," Tooms growled.

Shorty ignored him. And he ignored the sparks of anger in Goldie Vale's eyes. He got painfully to his feet and glared at them. Once again he was the little man on a short fuse. Unable to lift his arms more than a few inches from his sides, unable to speak much louder than a whisper, he raked them up and down with his anger.

"Well, Mrs. Courtney, what do you say?"

Her hands fluttered like pale moths. "Nothing . . . What more could I tell you?"

"For once," he said, as if he were biting bullets, "why don't you try the truth?"

She appealed with washed-out eyes to Tooms and Goldie. "Ma'am," he hissed, as a bullet hisses through thin air, "maybe you never cared for your husband when he was alive, and maybe you don't care now that he's dead. But I do. Somehow it's all tied up with an old sheepman that saved my hide not far back. It's tied up with a drygulch rifleman that nigh took my head right off my shoulders. It's tied up with a job that I lost, and a mail pouch, too, and a shack that was burned down, as well as Goldie's saloon. Not to mention several head of dead, half-burned sheep and a mule, and a whole town sick and dyin' with the after effects of lynch fever. So you can see that I ain't just talkin' to hear my head rattle—I want to hear the truth."

The woman looked stunned by his outburst.

"Ma'am!" he said, the one word cracking like a pistol shot.

She seemed to crumble. It began with her face, slowly folding, like a wax mask slowly melting. It extended to her eyes, and her slumping shoulders, and her heavy-hanging head, and finally to the spirit that was inside her. "It was the boy," she said wearily. "He was the one at the bottom of it."

"Vance English?"

She nodded.

"What about him?" Now Tooms and Goldie were watching and listening intently.

"I'm not sure," the Widow Courtney said bleakly. "I didn't read all the report. But it was John English's son. I think it was a case of murder."

Shorty breathed in as much air as his constricted lungs would hold. "Who was it he murdered?"

She shook her head slowly. "Someone named Ramon."

Shorty let his breath out with a sighing sound. Ramon. He was not particularly surprised—Vance had been the kind who would have shot a sheepman just for the sport of the thing, as old Bohannan had said.

Still, Ramon had only been the son of a mutton puncher—could the killing of one such man worry the ranchers so? "What," he asked, "made this Ramon so important?"

She looked at him blankly.

Shorty said, "It ain't like this was the first time a sheepman wound up in a gulley with a bullet in his back. What was it that caused all the fuss?"

She shook her head dumbly, and Shorty couldn't even be sure that she had heard him. "Ma'am," Shorty started in a tone as cold as Toledo steel. But Tooms, peering through the barred window, held up a hand for silence. "We're about to have company."

The cell was suddenly tomb-quiet. Soon they all began to hear the sound of horsebackers—the creak of saddle leather, the silver rattle of bridle chains, the musical jangling of spurs. They heard the huffing of the animals, the dust-muted thudding of hoofs. In that silence of a deserted town in early morning, every small noise was distinct and clear, spidery lines of sounds black-etched on the steely day.

"Maybe it's Dodd comin' with help," Goldie ventured.

Tooms turned to his window and Shorty to the street-side loophole, putting aside wishful thinking.

"How many you make it?" Shorty asked.

"Maybe a dozen," Tooms grunted, "from the racket they're makin'."

The horsemen had entered the town somewhere near the wagon yard, keeping the line of business houses between themselves and the jail. Now they reined up a little past Phil Sublet's saloon. An excited murmuring drifted like smoke through the narrow alleyways and around corners of buildings.

"I guess," Tooms said, "this is where Nate Corry gives old English his side of the story."

"Vance is dead—at least that much is true. John English won't care about anything else."

"Maybe it was a mistake lettin' Corry go," Goldie said. "He'll just whip them up in a killin' mood."

Shorty didn't bother to answer her. It was a sure thing that English had been in a killing mood for several hours.

Tooms glanced over his shoulder at the women, and his voice and his eyes were worried. "The old man's goin' to be in a mean way, all right. But somehow I

192

can't see him shootin' a woman."

Goldie Vale shrugged, as if they were discussing someone else in some other line of trouble, far away. "Maybe. But Nate Corry would if it meant savin' his own hide."

Mrs. Courtney stared at them in panic. "There's just the two of you," she said accusingly, "and maybe twelve of them!"

"I can handle a gun as good as most cowhands," Goldie said.

But the Widow Courtney gave no sign of hearing her. "That other man, Dodd, he'll never bring help." And now she was frankly whining. "He never aimed to come back; he just wanted to get away with his whole skin. I never should of listened to you. I should of run, like all the others. I would have been safe now, if I hadn't listened to you."

Shorty was fascinated and grimly amused at the subtle play of emotions in the marshal's face. Anger, pity, sympathy, outrage—they all darted and flitted behind those slitted eyes. "Ma'am," he said stiffly, "I wouldn't want to hold you here if you figure you'd be safer somewheres else."

Once again those pale hands fluttered like falling butterflies. She was far beyond thinking; she could only react to panic. "We'll all be killed!" she cried. "We'll all be killed . . ." But she made no move to leave the jail. Instead she sank down in the corner, wringing her hands. Then, abruptly, the muzzle blast of a rifle thoroughly shattered the fragile morning.

A heavy lead slug whipped through the loophole near Shorty's head and smashed itself flat against the opposite wall. Suddenly there was no time left for dealing with vacillating widows.

3

Out of the taut stillness that followed the first shot John English called, "Tooms! Hoyt Tooms, do you hear me?"

Shorty heard the marshal sigh. "Keep watch toward the back," he said quietly to Goldie; "the old man might have some of his hands come at us out of the weeds." Then he called in an unruffled, almost-conversational tone, "We hear you, English."

"Where's my boy, Marshal?" The words were as jagged as pieces of broken glass.

"Where he fell," Tooms answered dully. "Over there in the weeds, not far from the back of O'Dell's. There wasn't time to do anything about him—we kind of figured you and your hands would come pretty fast when you heard." He paused. "I guess Corry's already told you his side of it."

"He has." It might have been a hundred-year old speaking. Very old and very tired and sick with grief, and every atom of his being poisoned with hate.

Tooms ducked and moved to the grain-sack breastworks. "You see anything?" he asked Shorty.

"Not yet. But English is over at the side of O'Dell's.

194

I figure he's sent some of his hands to sharpshoot from the roofs."

Nobody mentioned Charlie Dodd or the possibility of help. That hope had pretty well vanished, along with other dreams and foolish wishes that grow in the night.

"Which one of you killed my boy?" John English called, with the bleakness of a prairie winter. "Corry claims it was the mail rider, Gibbs."

"For once in his life," Shorty called, louder than he had intended, "your foreman ain't lyin'. The truth is, English, that Vance needed killin'. Maybe somebody ought to of done it a long time ago and saved this country a deal of grief."

Tooms whipped around and glared angrily. "If he wasn't in a killin' mood before, he sure is now!"

Shorty snorted. "Once in his lifetime, every man ought to hear the truth, even old bulls like John English."

A bullet whanged against the rock wall, and another burned over the grain-sack barricade and straight out through the barred window. Somehow, Shorty thought to himself, this calaboose don't seem as safe as it did when we was fixin' it out to be a fort! He gestured for the women to get down on the floor against the walls. But the widow was already down, huddled in the corner, and Goldie baldly ignored the warning, keeping watch at the rear loophole.

"Where the hell are they?" Shorty snarled to no one in particular.

The icy voice of John English broke the uneasy silence. "Listen to me, Tooms. It ain't you we want, and it ain't the women. It's Gibbs that I aim to see dead before this day is out. Are you goin' to make us kill the bunch of you to get at him? Or will you turn him over to us now?"

The marshal turned slowly and faced Shorty with an unpleasant grin. "It might just be," he murmured, "that I'll never get a better proposition." But when he shouted back to the rancher, it was in a different tone. "We're not goin' to strike any bargains, English. If you figure you can dig us out of this calaboose, come ahead . . . but your boy won't be the only dead Spur hand when it's over."

"All right, Tooms." The old cowman sounded as if he were choking. "Have it your own way."

He must have given a signal. A dozen rifles cracked at almost the same instant. Lead slugs smashed against the stone of the calaboose, spraying the area with grit and dust. One bullet found its way through Shorty's loophole and ricocheted halfway around the inside of the jail before thudding into a grain sack. Shorty glanced around and saw Tooms gazing with dim interest at a shallow furrow in his left arm. "Ricochet," he said thoughtfully. "That's somethin' I hadn't counted on."

With blood dripping from his elbow, the marshal removed some grain sacks from the base of the breastworks and put them on top to narrow the opening. Working methodically, with the hail of rifle slugs still assaulting the stone walls, he wedged a sack of corn into each of the two loopholes. "That won't give them quite so much to shoot at."

The firing slacked off and finally stopped. Without a word, Goldie left her watch for a few moments, ripped off the sleeve of the marshal's shirt and fashioned a bandage around the shallow wound. Tooms, peering over his barricade, hardly seemed to notice.

"You see anything?" he asked Shorty.

"Just some powder smoke, so far."

English had posted some of his men on the far slopes of the pitched roofs, and others in narrow alleyways between buildings, flanking the jail. Luckily, the angle of fire was not great enough to allow the rooftop riflemen to shoot at them through the roofless top of the calaboose.

Silence dangled in empty air. English was giving them time to ponder the fix they were in. But when the rancher spoke again, it was not to gloat or threaten.

"Tooms . . . I want to get my boy."

The marshal turned and looked at Shorty, and Shorty nodded.

"English ain't no shorthorn," the marshal said. "He knows more tricks than a bitch coyote with a den full of pups."

"Just the same, Vance was his boy. Let the old man take him."

Tooms gazed at him with an air of speculation. One minute thirsting for blood, the next minute agreeing to give English the run of the place. Gibbs was not an easy man to figure. "All right, English," the marshal called. "Take the boy."

They listened to the vague sounds of troops moving into new positions. "At least," Shorty said to the others, "it'll give us a breathin' spell." And time to think, he thought to himself. And maybe even time to pray a little, if any of us knows how.

John English moved into the open from behind O'Dell's store. Naked of weapons, stiff as a ramrod, an old man burning bright with fires of his own making, he tramped across the broad back alley without so much as a sidelong glance in the direction of the jail. Close behind him, and obviously nervous, came Sam Milo, the Association man.

Shorty watched with curious emptiness as that short, sad procession headed for the thick green stand of mullein where Vance's body lay. For most of his grief, Shorty told himself, the old man had only himself to blame. Outlaw horses didn't get born outlaws, they were made that way when they were colts—and he guessed that humans weren't so much different.

Now English, standing hip deep in the dark green weeds, stared starkly down at what had been his son. And Shorty Gibbs, for one, was suddenly sick of the whole affair. Even his anger went cold.

Then a voice that Shorty failed to recognize immediately, taut, eager, expectant, hissed almost in his ear. "What are you waiting on! *Kill him!*"

Startled, Shorty twisted suddenly, and the knives

gouged savagely at his innards. The Widow Courtney had come to her feet and was peering over the top of the marshal's breastworks. Her eyes glittered and her voice shook with impatience.

"What's the matter with you!" She stared wildly at their faces. "Can't you see this is our only chance to save ourselves? Kill John English—we'll have nothing to fear from the others!"

The marshal's face remained blank but his voice was dark, "I told him he could take his boy, Mrs. Courtney. He's got my word."

"Your *word.*" She sounded incredulous. She sounded and looked as if she could not believe that a man would continue to stand by his word when his life was threatened. What a wife she must have made for Courtney, Shorty thought to himself. How little she must have known about the man and the business he had worked at. "What does your word mean," she demanded, "when our lives are at stake!"

"It means somethin' to me, ma'am."

The widow turned in desperation to Goldie. "Miss Vale, talk to him, make him see reason!"

Goldie stared at her. "Ma'am, there's nothin' I could say that would change his mind. Besides, I happen to agree with him."

Stunned, Mrs. Courtney turned to Shorty. "Mr. Gibbs, you're a reasonable man; can't you make them . . ."

But Shorty was already shaking his head, not risking himself to speak.

The widow flared in anger. "Won't any of you do anything!"

"Yes, ma'am," Tooms rumbled softly. "We'll set and we'll wait for old English to take his boy and lay him out, or whatever he feels like doin'. And then, unless we get a new run of luck, I guess we'll go on with the war."

4

English and Sam Milo returned from the weed patch carrying Vance's body between them. First in disbelief and then in panic, Mrs. Courtney watched their chance for survival being ignored—as she was being ignored.

"Marshal Tooms!"

Tooms gazed blandly straight ahead.

"Mr. Gibbs!"

"Ma'am," Tooms said at last, with ponderous politeness, "I don't expect it'll be long now before the trouble starts. You'll be safer down on the floor where you was before."

She was beaten. They put her out of their minds, as though she herself had suddenly vanished from that stone enclosure.

As they returned with the body, Sam Milo darted frightened glances in the direction of the jail, but John English stared with dry-eyed fierceness straight ahead. Shorty deliberately turned his thought to other things. A neutral sun rose in a summer sky, and he thought of Charlie Dodd with a shrug of resignation. Well, it had been a last-ditch hope anyway, cowman turning against cowman.

Shorty thought he saw something move along the ridge of a pitched roof. "I think the war's about to commence again."

Sure enough, English called from the far side of the general store, his words as hard as stones. "Tooms, I haven't changed my mind about anything."

"I didn't expect you would," the marshal answered.

"You still won't turn Gibbs over to us!"

"That's right." But before saying it, Tooms had turned and grinned his catlike grin at Shorty.

"He's a murderer, Tooms. Why get yourself killed on account of a murderer?"

"I'll let the county authorities worry that out for theirselves."

"He's goin' to die, Marshal. Today. By hisself at the end of my saddle rope. Or by a bullet, along with the rest of you. One way or the other."

"English," the marshal suddenly snarled, "you've been king of the hill too long. I always figured the day would come when I'd have to stand up to you—all right, this is the day!"

A bullet whanged into the calaboose, spraying gritty dust in Shorty's face. It was almost a relief to have the shooting started again.

Shorty and Tooms held their fire until they had something definite to shoot at. Meanwhile, bullets peppered the walls of the calaboose and thudded into the heavy grain sacks. Another lethal cone of lead whipped through the opening near Shorty's head, this time smashing flat against the opposite wall, missing Goldie by inches.

Goldie angrily brushed away the grayish dust that had showered her hair. "Sure enough," she said, "some of the Spur bunch is comin' up through the weed patch."

Tooms turned, looking as worried. "How many?"

Goldie shrugged. "Two, maybe three."

"They're gettin' at us from three sides," Shorty muttered. "This damn calaboose of yours, Marshal, is beginnin' to feel more like a trap than a fort." He faced the marshal with a sour grin. "I'm a fresh air man, myself. Never took much to closed-in places. So if you'll just nudge some of them grain sacks to one side, I think I'll strike out for somewheres else."

"Gibbs," Tooms said wearily, "I know you're bullheaded and maybe some saddle galled from the way English has been ridin' you, but you ain't no fool. And you're too runty to make a hero. So forget about walkin' out into that cross fire."

CHAPTER ELEVEN

1

Goldie Vale eased the sudden silence by taking the marshal's spare rifle, aiming briefly through the rear loophole and giving the trigger a slow, professional-like squeeze. The sound inside the close stone walls was ear-punishing and violent, but not so deafening that they couldn't hear the yell of pain from that green sea of mullein. Goldie had drawn first blood.

Shorty grinned stiffly and turned back to his own loophole. His attempt to walk out into that bullet-swept alley had been a fool thing to try. It had looked like a grandstand play, and maybe it had been just that.

But at the time he had been sure of one thing—and still was. This rock wall sense of security was a false one. Sooner or later a bullet would find its mark, and more than likely sooner. English had the men and the time and the ammunition. And it looked like Dodd wouldn't be returning. One thing was sure; the Hardrow citizenry wouldn't be digging itself out of the washes and gullies until the fight was over.

For most of the night a single thought had been plaguing him—Shorty Gibbs had killed Vance, and Shorty Gibbs was the one the old man wanted. Not the others. What right did he have to endanger their lives?

Goldie was watching him narrowly. Sensing it,

Shorty turned and stared into those slitted green eyes. "Vance is dead," she told him, "but that hasn't really changed anything. The thing that prodded Vance into killing is now proddin' the old man. You walk out of here and it means he'll have just one man to fight instead of two."

In anger and frustration Shorty wheeled and fired his .45 at a targetless rooftop.

Now, in a sudden lull, they all heard it. "Horses," Shorty said, but not with any hope. "Two, maybe three. If it's Dodd, he's bringin' mighty little help."

Horsebackers, three of them, were riding in from the South. Shorty caught glimpses of them between the buildings, and he groaned to himself in dismay. It *was* Dodd. And he had with him the two ranchers, Straiter and Maston. Two old men and them not even armed!

"A big help," Tooms said in cold anger, "that Association man turned out to be."

Well, Shorty thought, it had been a longshot chance at best. Under his breath he said, "It's a wonder English ain't shot them right out of their saddles."

"I sure hope," Tooms worried, "that Maston and Straiter brought some of their hands along. Maybe they're leavin' them out of town a piece, until they see for theirselves what kind of temper English is in."

Shorty snorted. "Maybe Dodd was able to talk sense to the old cowmen, but it looks like their hands just wasn't in no mood to make war on the Spur . . . still, it don't make much sense for Straiter and Maston to ride into a trap this way. Unless they figured they can *reason* with English." In which case, he thought, it's apt to be the last figurin' they'll ever do.

There was a flurry of activity in hidden places. The horsebackers were out of sight for a little while on the far side of the buildings. Then they slanted directly into the alley. Two Spur hands hustled out of hiding to keep the horsemen covered with rifles.

There was hardly a sound, except for the huffing of the horses and the patient thudding of hoofs on hard clay. Then, as the trio put themselves between the Spur riflemen and the jail, English called, "That's far enough."

The horsebackers reined to a stop just where the old cowman wanted them, directly in the line of fire. English moved slowly into the open but Shorty caught only a glimpse of his boots beneath the bellies of the horses. "Hold up on the shootin'," Tooms said, "till we see where everybody stands."

"You're an Association man, I hear," English was saying icily to Dodd. "I want to know what you're doin' in Hardrow."

Shorty noticed that all three horsebackers had come unarmed. He groaned. If they thought *that* was going to save them, they were fools.

Stone-faced, Charlie Dodd was saying, "I ride for the Association, like Ralph Courtney used to do. I'm here on business."

When English spoke again his voice was still coldly impersonal, but Shorty got the feeling that he was worried. "You brought company, I see," finally recognizing the presence of Straiter and Maston.

Straiter started to speak, but Dodd cut in ahead of him. "They're on business too," he said. "Cow business, the same as yours, Mr. English. But Mr. Straiter and Mr. Maston want to *stay* in the cow business."

Charlie Dodd slouched forward in the saddle. He pushed his hat back and considered the situation. "Mr. English," he said at last, "I know about your boy, and I'm sorry. I can even understand how you feel—like there's fire in your gut and gall in your mouth, and the only thing you can think about is bustin' things up and killin' somebody."

"Damn you, Dodd . . ." English started.

Dodd came suddenly erect, glaring. "Hear me out, English." They were suddenly equals—it was no longer "Mr." when Dodd addressed the old cowman. "Just listen to me. Then you can let your men shoot me out of the saddle . . ." He shrugged. "If you just won't be satisfied until you get Rangers up here ridin' herd on every cowman in the Panhandle."

He let that galling thought simmer. "Do you think," he asked harshly, "that you're the only father that ever felt his guts on fire because he lost a son? Maybe you never heard about an old sheepman named Bohannan."

Shorty tensed and wished that he could see the old cowman's face.

Dodd went on. "It's kind of a long story, English. And an old one to some of you old-timers. Bohannan's boy was shot down for no better reason than he was a mutton puncher. It would be great sport, Vance figured, to shoot hisself a sheepman. And why not? After all, he was the son of John English, wasn't he? He could do anything that happened to strike his fancy, couldn't he? Nobody could do anything to a boy of John English." Dodd gazed bleakly at the cowman's face. "That's where Vance was wrong. And that's where you're wrong now, if you think Texas law don't reach all the way up to the Panhandle."

English's voice broke on the sudden stillness like hissing steam. "You're a liar, Dodd! And don't think I won't report this to your bosses in Fort Worth!" But the Association man only smiled, which made the old cowman even wilder. "I'll have your hide, Dodd. Maybe today, maybe a minute from now, or even sooner. Mister, the Panhandle is my private battleground, if I want to make it that. My word's the law here. So don't threaten me with Rangers. And don't come to me with stories about Vance. Not today!"

Paul Maston's animal sidestepped nervously, perhaps sensing the tenseness in the air. Now they could see English from the jail, but not his Spur hands who still had the horsebackers and the calaboose covered with rifles.

"You never heard of Seth Bohannan?" Dodd asked quietly. The old man, a drawn .45 in his hand, seemed to tower in his rage.

"Like I said," Dodd continued gently, "you ain't the only one to feel that fire in your gut. Bohannan's boy had been killed; he had to do somethin' about it. He started by writin' letters. He wrote the governor. He wrote to peace officers he'd met or heard about. He wrote to some rich Mex pals of his over in the New Mexico country. And he wrote the Association. Lord," Dodd sighed, "the letters that old man wrote!"

"Nobody listens to a mutton puncher," English rasped.

Dodd smiled his tight smile. "There's a lot of Texas south of the Cap Rock. There's railroaders and businessmen that want to see the Panhandle settled. There's farmers achin' to get a plow in this grassland. They all vote. The politicians are beginnin' to hear them when they holler. And that old man, Bohannan, hollered loud."

Shorty shot a look at Tooms. The big marshal shook his head hopelessly. "Dodd's just talkin' hisself into a quick grave."

The Association man continued patiently, "What I'm tryin' to say, English, is you're not lord of the Panhandle any more. You break the law and you have to answer for it like anybody else."

The old man's voice was thin and cold. "It ain't against no law to hang a murderer."

"Unless you're a Texas court, it is." Dodd moved one shoulder in a suggestion of resignation. "You're in this thing alone. You'll get no help from the Association or the other cowmen." Suddenly he snarled. "Can't you get it through your head that anything a cowman does to rile the public is goin' to make it that much harder on *all* cowmen?"

"What I know," English said with unmistakable finality, "is that I had a boy yesterday. Today I don't." He glared his hatred at the mounted ranchers. "I had friends yesterday. But not anymore."

He wheeled and started back to his waiting army. But Charlie Dodd had one more card to play. "I know," he said softly, "that Vance bushwhacked the mail rider and took his pouch. And I know that your foreman rode south the same day and held up the Fort Worth stage, takin' another mail pouch. Both of those pouches contained copies of Courtney's Association report—don't that strike you as kind of interestin'?"

The old man froze. "That's a lie!"

Dodd's voice turned bland. "I can prove it all in a court of law. I've been talkin' to Straiter and Maston. They're not in any hurry to start a shootin' war on Vance's account. They'll take the witness stand, if they have to, and tell the truth about the way Ramon Bohannan was murdered."

"You'll die for this! All of you!" English's voice was suddenly shrill.

"Maybe, but it won't change anything. The other cowmen will fight if they have to—and they'd rather fight you than the Rangers." He leaned forward in the saddle. "There's twenty armed men just outside of town, English. They've got their orders to settle this thing, no matter what happens to us."

English didn't believe it. Inside the calaboose, Tooms shook his head worriedly. "More gall than a bull buffalo. But it's just goin' to get him killed!"

Dodd went on in what was almost a conversational tone. "You know, English, there's mighty few secrets in range country. And murder's a hard thing to keep quiet—even the murder of a sheepman—when a man likes to talk as much as Vance did." He moved a hand in a gesture of hopelessness. "Why don't you let it drop, English? Don't make things worse than they already are."

But the old man had gone as rigid as a mountain of ice, and as deaf. In his mind he knew that the day of the cow god was passing. In his mind he knew that the Association had had no choice about investigating the killing of the Bohannan boy. Signs of the changing times were all around him; cowmen could no longer sweep their dirt under the rug, like in the old days. Getting away with murder, even of a single sheepman, was a thing of the past.

All these things he knew and acknowledged in his mind—but in his heart and guts he knew only that he had lost his son.

The thin outer layer of the old cowman's mind was aware of Dodd's voice droning on in the desperate hope that he could outtalk a father's lust for vengeance.

Something about coal oil. Dodd was saying there had been the smell of oil at the various fires; at the saloon, at Shorty's shack, at Bohannan's burned camp, and finally he had discovered the same smell on Vance's riding gear when he had rounded up the horses that night. As if all this talk of oil and fire could fill the emptiness in an old man's heart.

There was something about the Association detective, Courtney, and something about Vance getting the mob whipped up that night of the lynching. It barely touched the old man's consciousness.

Inside the calaboose, Shorty said grimly, "English ain't even listenin'. It don't make a bit of difference to him whether Vance was guilty or innocent. He's too busy thinkin' up the best and slowest way of killin' the bunch of us."

Then a lone, awkwardly hopping, lurching figure appeared on the far side of O'Dell's. Nate Corry, using a rifle for a crutch, was flinging himself across the broad alley toward John English.

"He's a bald-faced liar!" the foreman shouted, leaving a trail of blood behind him as his bandage worked itself loose. "That Association man was right alongside Gibbs when Gibbs killed Vance."

English stood as rigid as ice sculpture.

Nate Corry, leaning hard on the rifle, had made his way to his boss. "Don't listen to him, Mr. English. He's just tryin' to rattle you!"

The old cowman turned on him in cold hatred. "You was supposed to see that nothin' happened to my boy. Get out of my sight. I don't want to lay eyes on you again."

Nate was stunned. Then he paled with anger. "Look here, Mr. English, you ain't hardly in any way to tell me . . ."

English hit him with barrel of his drawn revolver. It

was a savage, powerful blow that sent Corry reeling back, the rifle-crutch flying from his grasp. He fell sprawling on the stonelike ground, sheet-white with pain and rage.

Filth and obscenity were on the top of the foreman's tongue, but with tremendous will he bit them off.

"It's the truth!" he said to Dodd with vicious pleasure. "Vance killed that kid mutton puncher. Murdered him. Shot him down and laughed about it." He shifted his anger back to his boss. "That's the kind of boy you had, Mr. English. That's the way Vance really was."

"Shut up!" the old man shouted.

Corry grinned with pale lips. "You never ought to of knocked me down, Mr. English. After all the things I've done for you and that whelp of yours."

There was frank sadistic glee in Corry's eyes. "Shut up," John English said again in a choked voice, "or I'll kill you where you lay."

"And he'll do it," Shorty Gibbs said to the calaboose wall, "if somebody don't stop him."

Tooms shot him a slitted look. "If Nate wants to get hisself killed, it's all right with me."

"Like I always thought," Shorty snarled, "a ton of blubber don't make a marshal. Dodd's bluffin'! I'll bet a Christmas orange against that tin badge that Straiter and Maston didn't bring a single man with them." He shook his head angrily. "If English kills Corry, he'll be killin' the only man alive that can give a first hand account of what really happened."

And Corry seemed intent on getting himself killed.

Perhaps the years of playing nursemaid to Vance had built up mountains of frustration that could not be leveled by mere reason. He had glimpsed pain in the old man's eyes, and seeing it had given him pleasure.

"Yes sir," Shorty muttered, "Corry's just about good as dead." He wheeled on Tooms. "Heave some of that corn out of the way. I want out of here!"

Tooms stared. "You gone loco?"

Shorty pointed his .45 at the blocked doorway and fired. The bullet tore into the corner of a grain sack and loose corn dribbled slowly onto the floor. Shorty looked at Tooms. "I could shoot my way out, like that, but it would take more time than I want to spend. And it would take more time than Corry's got for livin'."

Pinpoints of light appeared in the marshal's eyes. He was beginning to understand that, at that moment, Shorty Gibbs was the only man that John English hated more than the foreman, and the only one capable of turning the old cowman's hate from Corry.

"All right," Tooms grated, "if you just *got* to get yourself shot." He grabbed a sack of corn in his huge hands and opened a narrow gap next to the doorframe.

Goldie made a small, helpless sound as she turned and saw Shorty squeeze through the opening. "Shorty, don't be a fool!"

Little late, he thought, to be worryin' about that. He took a few steps from the jail and shouted, "I'm the one you're lookin' for, English. *I'm* the one that shot Vance."

It took the old man a moment to redirect his hate. Charlie Dodd expertly nudged his animal out of the line of fire. The hail of bullets that Shorty had half-expected did not come. Instead, a tightly drawn silence fell over the shabby battlefield. The Spur hands, by their silence, were observing the old man's desire for personal satisfaction. They were only cowhands, after all.

John English turned from the foreman with his .45 in his hand, cocked ready for killing. Shorty ignored the knives gouging at his insides. He cocked his own revolver.

"English, it don't have to be this way. Let the law handle it."

The old cowman grinned—but on that weathered face it was an expression of hatred. He could see only one thing: the man who had killed his son.

Then, into that astringent silence, someone shouted. Shorty realized later that it was Tooms, but at the moment he heard only a wordless, anxious sound, the briefest instant before a rifle cracked.

The next instant Nate Corry was spread-eagled on the ground, thoroughly dead, as if some invisible spike had been driven through his body.

Two rifles spoke almost at once, one from the jail and one from the roof of O'Dell's store. It seemed that an invisible hand grasped John English by the shoulder, spun him around and slammed him to the ground. Almost a hundred yards from the spot, Shorty Gibbs, without firing a shot, watched Sam Milo roll down the shingled slope and thud to the ground.

Then it seemed that everybody was shooting, and Shorty suddenly found himself on the ground watching with stunned unreality as bright crimson spread over his shirtfront. That's *my* blood, he thought silently.

2

Shorty returned to the world with the air of a man who is surprised to find himself still alive. He looked around and recognized the interior of the marshal's shack. He had slept and bled on the marshal's bunk.

He looked up and saw Goldie Vale's faintly sardonic grin. "Is the war over?"

"Lasted just long enough for you to get yourself shot in the shoulder. Then the crews from the Maston and Straiter outfits galloped into town and the Spur men seemed to lose heart." She held something to his mouth; whiskey. He downed it in a single gulp.

"You mean," he said when he got his breath, "that Dodd actually did bring help? He wasn't just bluffin'?" It was hard to believe. "Is John English dead?"

She shook her head. "Just winged by Sam Milo."

Shorty let this knowledge roll in his mind. He dimly remembered seeing Milo drygulch Corry—because Milo couldn't afford to let the foreman tell all he knew about his connection with English and the murders, no doubt. Then Milo had tried to kill English for the same reason . . .

In the midst of that thought Shorty Gibbs went to sleep.

When he opened his eyes again, the coal-oil lamp was burning and Tooms was in the room looking down at him. "How long have I been asleep?"

"Twelve hours, more or less," the marshal said with an ill-tempered edge.

Twelve hours! His shoulder throbbed and was heavily bandaged, but he could still move it. No bones broken. He asked at last. "Is it all over?"

"It's over, but the Panhandle will never be the same."

"I forgot about Milo when I stepped outside that calaboose," Shorty said. "That was a mistake."

"And not your only one," Tooms said bitingly. He pulled up a dried apple crate and sat and stared bleakly at Shorty Gibbs. "But you was right about Corry. He was the only one that could of set everything straight. That's why Sam Milo had to kill him, I guess, when he seen the foreman had been prodded into tellin' everything he knew. But tryin' to kill John English was a poor move. The old man never would of told anything that would hurt the English name."

Shorty lay still for a moment. "Is Goldie all right?"

The marshal nodded and asked, "How soon do you aim to leave Hardrow?"

"As soon as I can set a saddle," Shorty said with feeling.

216

Tooms stared at the far wall. "I've been thinkin'. Maybe you ought to take Goldie with you."

Shorty came half-off the bunk and fell back gasping.

"It was just a notion," Tooms said blandly. He rose ponderously to his feet and tramped out.

Late that afternoon Charlie Dodd stopped by. He had a roll under his arm and the look of a man bent on traveling. "You pullin' out already?" Shorty asked dryly. "You figure you got all the answers?"

"All the answers—but not much satisfaction." He sat on the edge of the bunk, his face gray and drawn. "Ralph Courtney," he said, "dead. Vance English, Milo, Nate Corry, old Bohannan and his boy Ramon—all dead. And for nothin'." The Association detective looked angry and tired. "How much has the marshal told you?" he asked.

"Whatever he figured was good for me, I guess."

Dodd shrugged. "All this killin' could of been avoided if John English had took a razor strop to Vance fifteen years ago . . ." But that was wishful thinking and not in a range detective's line. He went on. "Out of high spirits and bad liquor, Vance killed Ramon Bohannan. All the ranchers knowed about it— they didn't approve of it, exactly, but they didn't worry much about it either. Not at first. But they hadn't counted on Bohannan raisin' so much hell about it, stirring up the politicians down at Austin. Startin' the farmers to thinkin' about all this free land in the Panhandle."

Dodd gazed bleakly at nothing. "It must of come as

a big shock to the cowmen," he said, "when them leather-lunged politicians started hollerin' murder, and the rest of Texas started believin' it. All because of one young mutton puncher. All of a sudden the cowman was gettin' hisself a bad name. All of a sudden he realized he was in a good way of losin' the last free grass in Texas, if somethin' wasn't done. Even their own Association, the outfit that men like English and Straiter and Maston had created in the first place, had turned against them. All except Sam Milo, who was on the Spur payroll."

"What about that piece of envelope that you found at Bohannan's wagon?" Shorty asked, skipping everything that didn't directly affect the fortunes of Shorty Gibbs.

Dodd shook his head. "I'm comin' to it. Vance had roped Sam Milo into his scheme to get hold of that report. Milo knew all about Association routine. Some of his pals in Fort Worth told him about the investigation, and he told Vance and the old man. Anyhow, Milo kept tabs on Courtney until he found out when the report was bein' mailed. You know the rest. Corry rode south to hold up the stage and take the Association copy. Vance waited for you at Gyp Creek and left you for dead."

Shorty nodded. "And he opened the report on the spot and dropped the envelope, where Bohannan found it at the same time he found me."

"That's how it looks."

"You got the answers, all right," Shorty said wryly.

"Somebody's been doin' some fast talkin'."

Dodd smiled without humor. "Maston and Straiter. They told it the way they heard it from John English at the time when English thought they were goin' to fight this out together. Maston and Straiter wasn't so particular as long as they figured cowmen was still kings of the Panhandle. Now they're all for law and order and cooperatin' with the Association."

Shorty made a sound in his throat that Dodd chose to ignore. "Anyhow," he continued, "Vance knowed that Courtney could always write another report, long as he was alive. And Ralph, bein' the curious bird he was, played right into Vance's hands by comin' to Hardrow for some extra snoopin'. And got hisself hung."

He sat for a moment in angry silence. Courtney was dead for just one reason—he had taken his job too much to heart.

"Then come Mrs. Courtney," Shorty said. "I seen Vance all but shoot her off that one-horse rig of hers, but nobody would believe me."

"I believe you now," Dodd said. "And so do Straiter and Maston and Tooms, and maybe even John English. If it matters."

Shorty lay for a while in thought. Even before he had come to Hardrow the old-time cattle kings had started losing their grip. Settlement of the Panhandle had already been a sure thing; the killing of Ramon had only roused people and brought it about a little sooner than anybody had expected.

Shorty's thoughts drifted. It was all over. The Spur hands, after all, were only cowhands, not soldiers. An old man's vendetta didn't mean anything to them.

"What about Courtney's widow?" Shorty asked after a long silence. "Did she really take money to keep quiet about the lynchin'?"

Again Dodd's mouth stretched in a humorless smile. "I don't guess anybody thought to ask before she left."

Shorty blinked. "She's gone?"

"Back to stay with folks she knows in Tascosa. Fixin' her rig wasn't no big job, once I convinced the blacksmith he ought to work on it."

Shorty's instinct was toward anger. But somehow, maintaining an anger for a woman like Mrs. Courtney didn't seem to be worth the trouble. He closed his eyes and thought to himself, What do you know about it, Gibbs? You never was a woman, scared and rattled and all of a sudden throwed out on your own. So maybe this once you ought to keep your mouth shut.

"What's goin' to happen to John English?" he asked.

"That's up to the law now." Dodd started for the door. "Anything you want?"

Shorty thought for a minute. "Yes. I know in a general way why the cowmen wanted me out of the Panhandle, but I still can't get it through my head that it was worth killin' for."

"You could," Dodd said, "if you was English. The cowmen was in a way where they just couldn't stand bad publicity. And Shorty Gibbs was a loose, untidy end left dangling, a constant reminder to folks that they had lynched a man. All the unpleasantness focused on you, like heat comin' to focus through a burnin' glass. I guess the cowmen were scared that your hard-headedness would cause folks to do somethin' violent and draw even more attention to them."

His eyes closed, Shorty said, "And that's why English tried to buy me instead of killin' me—he was afraid another killin' would draw more attention from the politicians in Austin."

Dodd nodded. "There's one more thing. That report in your mail pouch was probably addressed to Sam Milo. It's the usual thing for an investigator like Courtney to send a report of his work to the Association man on the spot."

Shorty was quick to comprehend the meaning of that statement. With bitter irony, fate had turned on the cowmen, kicking them in the gut with their own arrogance. With one copy in Milo's hands, and Milo's pals in Fort Worth disposing of the other copy, it was at least conceivable that the old cowmen might have ridden out the storm. But when Vance had started acting on his own . . .

Dodd was standing by the door. Clearly he was tired of the whole business and wanted only to get away. "Well, Gibbs . . . Is there anything else?"

"No." Shorty was thinking about Tooms. The marshal could have prevented a lot of grief if he had done his duty the night they dragged Courtney out of the calaboose. But, then, Shorty thought, I don't really know what it feels like to stand up to my friends and maybe have to shoot them down in order to save one stranger, any more than I know what it feels like to be a widow.

Some time later he looked up and saw Goldie Vale watching him from the open doorway. There was a worn grip on the floor at her feet, and a small bundle of personal things in one hand.

"Just thought I'd stop to say good-by," she said.

Shorty squinted, surprised. "Where you goin'?"

She shrugged. "North, I guess. One of the cowtowns on the Western Trail. There's a peddler over at the wagon yard said he'd let me ride far as the Cimarron with him."

Despite the gouging knives, Shorty pushed himself up on the bunk. "Mighty little future in them hundred-day wonders they call cowtowns."

Again Goldie hunched her shoulders. "Saloon work's the only kind of work I know."

Shorty looked at her for what seemed a long time. "I been doin' some thinkin'," he said abruptly, almost angrily. "These cowmen like English, their time's run out. If they can't change, they're done for. I guess that goes for saloon girls, too. And ex-drovers." He grimaced, as if he had suddenly bitten into something bitter.

They studied each other with unclouded eyes. Fine pair *we'd* make, Shorty thought to himself. A female saloonkeeper without a saloon, and a stove-up drover out of a job.

"North," he said abruptly, with distaste. "No more of

them Kansas winters for me. But if you decide to head south, maybe we might as well travel together." He hesitated. "If you ain't in any hurry."

She looked at him steadily, and Shorty began to feel the heat of his discomfort rising in his face. I must be out of my head, he thought savagely, thinkin' that any woman with good sense would want to throw in with Shorty Gibbs. "Forget it!" he was about to say. Backing out of the awkward situation as gracefully as possible.

Goldie grinned at him and seemed to shrug. "I ain't in any special hurry."

Shorty lay back on the bunk. For a moment he felt like a blundering coon that had stuck its paw in a beartrap. Behind that grin of Goldie's he sensed a devious female wisdom at work.

Wisely, he decided not to tamper with it. Best start living with it now, he told himself, if this is the way it's going to be.

For a moment a disturbing vision of Goldie and himself flashed in his mind. Ahead of them he glimpsed a tortuously twisting road liberally strewn with bone-breaking boulders of their own hard-headedness.

But then, peering deeper into that vision, he saw stretches where the road was smooth and straight, and the going would not be hard.

Center Point Publishing
600 Brooks Road ● PO Box 1
Thorndike ME 04986-0001 USA

(207) 568-3717

**US & Canada:
1 800 929-9108**